GHOSTS ON VINTNERS LANDING

A Novel

By

Keith Gaddie

Printed in the United States of America.

Cataloging-in-Publication Data is available from the Library of Congress.

ISBN: 9780982675922
First edition, first printing.

Black Mesa Publishing, LLC
Florida
David Horne and Marc CB Maxwell
Black.Mesa.Publishing@gmail.com

"I never met a Kentuckian, anywhere around the world, who wasn't planning on going home some day."

Albert B. "Happy" Chandler
Former Governor of Kentucky

Prelude

HUMIDITY HUNG ON EVERYTHING, even on the light of the setting sun that shone through the doors opening onto the street corner. The heavy rays illuminated the dark woods of the bar and gave an orange hue to the red barstools. In the opposite corner of the bar, two waiters from one of the convention hotels were playing video poker. Two old locals, a retired mechanic and an old firefighter, held court at the bar with Jamie the bar maid, playing liar's poker and making wagers on the baseball game on the television sitting atop the glass-front Coke cooler full of beer. In the back dining room, the Mexican sandwich makers yelled orders to the waiting customers. Out in the street, a siren wailed in the distance, down toward Tchoupitoulas Street, and the faint yells of the evening streets coming to life echoed up Third Street.

The bar sat at the corner of Constance and Third Street in Uptown New Orleans. Once upon a time, it had been a grocery store. Then, it was a bar, and a restaurant. In the 1940s and 1950s, it had been one of a dozen or more neighborhood bars in the Irish Channel, each with their own loyal patrons who lived in the neighborhood. They had softball teams and bowling leagues and everyone in the bar knew everyone else, knew their kids, and knew each other's business. Each bar was an anchor for the blocks around it, back when the streets of New Orleans were safe at midnight and people left their kids outside without worry.

Then, later, when the Irish and Italians and Germans had fled New Orleans for the suburbs in Metairie and Chalmette, one by one the old neighborhood bars fell by the wayside. The whites – somehow the Italians and the Irish had become 'white' – came to the old neighborhood bars less often, not after work, not on Saturday night. One by one the taverns closed. Kerrigan's, Acey's, the '808', Dutch Koger's, Pete's Bar, Delaney's, one by one they all shuttered their doors as the crack wars took the streets of the Channel and the remaining white and black residents rode out the storm of drugs and violence that swept through the neighborhood in the late '80s and early '90s.

But this bar, this very one bar, it persisted. It survived the white flight, and the oil bust, and the gang wars, and even the big storm. The Saint Patrick's Day parade always made its way down to the corner and the old neighborhood always came to life for a day. The bar had rollicked through the drug wars and had invited in the renovators and young culture-jammers who took chances on renovating the old shotguns in the Channel. The big storm brought water, but only a foot or two, and only for a day. Now, with the waters gone, the Channel was one of the only neighborhoods of historic character that wasn't devastated. Every day, one or another of the old regulars made their way back, or the sons and daughters of old regulars, taking another chance on the old neighborhood after Katrina. And this was their bar.

Hayden walked in and took a seat at the stool nearest the door. Jamie came over to him, smiled, and sat a draft of thick, dark stout porter in front of him. It was his first time back since before the storm.

Jamie checked the two old locals, then went and flirted with the poker players for a few minutes, then went up in back to the kitchen. When she returned, she wiped down the bar and came to rest in front of Hayden.

"Well, we thought we'd lost you for good, Hayden. You back in New Orleans to stay?"

Hayden considered the beer, took a swallow, and set his eyes on the bartender. "Could be, Jamie. I came down to check on the house, and figured I'd drop in and have a drink. How'd the flood treat you?"

"Well enough. As good as could be expected," Jamie turned serious. "We lost the house down in the Marigney, but the bar here only took a foot of water. We were open the day after the National Guard let everyone back in town. You left before that, right?"

"Yeah, about six months before. After – "

Jamie remembered, regretting the question. She took his hand, held it. "Hey, I'm sorry babe. Totally forgot about that. But seems like you took an awfully long walk. Four years, I'd wager."

"That's be right, Jamie. Hey, set me up another one. And get Mr. Jake and Mr. Delmar down there too." Hayden finished the last of his pint. "It was four years, but it was a good walk. I had to get on down the line, take a look around. Funny thing about taking a walk – you always figure that you'll find your way over the horizon, but instead you find yourself on the way back home. And the most difficult ground to walk is the ground you figured you knew."

Jamie pulled the pints, and came back to Hayden. The old men hefted their glasses in appreciation toward Hayden, the silent, smiling nod of drinking men who appreciate the respect that accompanies a free pint at the end of a day.

"Y'know, Jamie, walking grounds you once knew, it's like trying to romance a woman again for the first time. You know what worked, once upon a time, and so does she. But now, you've both changed, you're older, you're wiser to each other and you've already loved each other, lost each other, and probably loved another. Love and loss changes you, and it makes it that much harder to romance each other again."

"So, have you been on the road for love? Or looking for something you lost?" Jamie smiled at him, the sad smile of a woman who favors damaged men. "Love and loss, love and loss. Hayden, you wield that sanguine tongue like a true Irishman. Tell you what, *cher*. I'm off in about an hour. You just sit tight, and I'll open a bottle of whiskey, and you can tell me your story. Tell me about love and loss, and then we'll compare notes. You tell me your tale. Maybe I'll tell you mine."

Hayden looked at her, a moment, two, considering his next thought. "Okay. It's not a tale from here, not from this place, but it does pass through here, through this place. Jamie, dear, I've spent my life running from ghosts, and chasing ghosts. So, draw me another pint, heft a bottle of bourbon, and then set your fair self beside me and I'll tell you a tale of a people so certain of their love that they'd inflict and endure any misery rather than express that love to each other. It's a story looking for its conclusion. But, I think I know how it ends, at least for a night."

An hour later, Jamie took off her apron and walked around from behind the bar. She took Hayden by the arm, and led him to the back of the little tavern, to a corner table beside the poker machines. She took a seat beside him, set two glasses down, and poured from a bottle of bourbon. Behind them, Mr. Jake glanced back over his shoulder, a twinkle in his grey eye as he looked back, remembering another time, another night, another young lady.

"Maybe, Hayden, maybe you've found the end of your tale, at least for tonight." Jamie raised her glass to his, her face smiling but her eyes wet with sympathy. "But *how* it ends, at least for a night, depends on if you tell the story right. Tell me your story, Hayden Rollin ... "

I. Prologue, Not Even Past

Keith Gaddie

Chapter 1

November 10, 1991
Vintners Landing, Kentucky

"HAYDEN? HAYDEN? WAKE UP HONEY."

"Huh? Five minutes. Just five minutes."

I eyeballed the clock and tried to shrink under the covers. 6:14 in the morning. Mom stood in the door, backlit by the hallway light.

"Nope. Sorry honey. Time to get you going. It isn't a dream. You really do have calculus in two hours."

Too early, I thought as I slouched into the bathroom and got a shower.

The sky was still dark outside when I walked into the kitchen. I had just discovered coffee. The dark winter weather was still around. A slow drizzle accompanied the cold air outside. I filled the Mr. Coffee, and then drowned some Cheerios in sugar and milk, and slumped over the kitchen table, not quite ready to make the thirteen-mile drive to the high school and start another day of differential equations and second order integrals. *I hated math*, I thought, *but they said I am good at it.*

It was about half past six. Dad had left for the office an hour before – the construction business starts the day early. The coffee brewed. Mom padded into the kitchen, in her old terry cloth robe, and turned on the radio to the 50,000 watt clear channel station from up in the city. The adult contemporary music ended. The legendary morning host took a happy phone call from Velma in Valley Station. Then a traffic report came on from the happy helicopter traffic tracker, followed by the news. The first story, I don't remember, but the second is burned on my memory:

> *"Daniel D. Cahill of Vintners Landing was killed this morning in an exchange of gunfire with police. The confrontation happened at three AM outside the Trattoria di la Vigna in the 600 block of Grapevine Road. Mr. Cahill, 18, had barricaded himself inside the restaurant after a family dispute. When the sheriff's office was called to the scene, Cahill fired on the deputies. He was killed by shots from the deputies who returned his fire."*

A cup dropped, clattering across the kitchen floor. I looked up from the table, across the kitchen toward my Mom. Her shocked expression mirrored my own, mouth agape and wide-eyed. Danny was dead, a violent death with a gun in his hand.

One of my first friends from childhood was dead with a bullet in his head. We both stood and stared. I didn't cry, nor did Mom. We just exhaled and got ready for the day.

Mom hopped in her Mercedes and headed toward Frankfort, to start another day of practicing law on behalf of the attorney general of Kentucky. I followed a few minutes later, headed for Carritherston and the high school.

The town where we lived, Vintners Landing, was one of the oldest settlements in Kentucky. Nestled on a turn of a tributary of the Kentucky River, twenty miles from Frankfort, Vintners Landing had grown up as a trading post back during the Revolutionary War. My mother's family, the Dixons, had come there before the war had even started, defying the British ban on white settlement west of the Allegheny Mountains. The little port had been called Dix's Port back then, but when great-grandpa's great-grandpa had decided to grow white grapes and make wine, the place received a new name – Vintner's Landing. Soon the landing and its tavern was a primary stopping place for the bargemen taking goods down the slow-moving Kentucky to the mighty Ohio River.

The Landing, as locals call it, is on the eastern edge of Cherokee County. The county runs along the west bank of the Kentucky River, and the county seat of Carritherston is due west of Vinters Landing along the L & N. Most of the business and government is over in the county seat, including the schools and the courthouse and the sheriff's office. The Dixons never left the east side of the county, at least not for any longer than to go to work or go to war, and neither did my daddy's family, the Rollins. This was where we were, this spot just off the river, uphill from Vintners Landing.

As I drove, I engaged in a mental sorting and shuffling habit that became part of my daily life – identifying the goals and problems before me; shuffling through them to figure out how I might deal with them; and then sorting them into parts of my brain to find solutions and put effort behind the problem. Usually this exercise was driven in part by alacrity or apprehension on my part to avoid the embarrassment of failure. On this morning, the needle reading the problems and challenges got stuck on one thought, an odd thought on which it kept skipping back to – that I had no emotional reaction or sense of loss in the death of a friend. The needle kept skipping on guilt.

I turned off the country lane leading out to the family farm, onto the Old Bard's Town Road and then onto Grapevine Road through Vintners Landing, To the right I saw where Danny had died. The Trattoria was still closed, of course, didn't open until just before lunch on weekdays. A sickening air hung about the place, like a still shadow that defied dawn's light. The engine on the old Mustang convertible roared to life as my foot depressed the accelerator, blowing the last of the cool November moisture out of the exhaust. Turning off Grapevine Road, I speeded down the Vintners Landing Road toward Carritherston. The only feeling I could find was disappointment, in myself, for not feeling any loss.

Chapter 2

KESSLER'S TRATTORIA DI LA VIGNA sat at the intersection of Kentucky 14 and Kentucky 44, on what locals called Grapevine Road. It was an unassuming building, sitting where the roads intersected and across from the railroad tracks, nestled between the old Stoneham house and the Esso Station. The building, faced with white-glazed ceramic brick, was two stories, the restaurant below and a rental office above. Off to the side of the storefront there was a porch, and at the end of the porch, a short walkway led to a small pump house. The paint on the siding was always fresh, no more than a summer or two old, eggshell blue finish, trimmed in white and green. Giant green, white, and red metal awnings hung over the windows and the porch. A faded sign above the second floor said "Kessler's."

The front entrance, an old wooden door with stained glass, was bracketed by a pair of large windows. Salamis and cheeses and gourds and garlic were hanging behind the glass. To the far side of the left window was an old 10-2-4 Dr. Pepper machine, the kind that held sodas behind a little glass door that you opened to pull out the bottle, busting your knuckles if you were not careful. Four rocking chairs sat on the porch, looking north toward the road and the railroad tracks that separated Grapevine Road from Hostel Street. Around to the right, on the side porch that led to storehouse, sat an ice chest.

When you opened the door, an old brass cowbell announced your entrance. The inside smelled of cheese and meat and herbs – garlic, oregano, basil – all of which lingered in the air. If you looked to the right, eight tables with little wicker-back chairs stood on the pinewood floors. Each of the eight little square tables was covered with a little red-and-white checked table cloth, and was surrounded by four walnut cane-bottom chairs. Each four-top had a bottle of olive oil, salt, pepper, a little metal napkin dispenser, oregano and parmesan, and a container of unsalted butter.

At the back of the room were two coolers full of soft drinks and a door that led to the restrooms. Looking to the left, running from the other front window to the back wall, ran a row of refrigerated display cases filled with Italian cheeses, Italian salamis and hams and sausages, and a few of the normal meat case products you'd expect to find at any country meat counter – ham, turkey, roasted beef, corn beef, and bologna. In Italy, they'd say that Kessler's was a *norcineria* – a seller of Italian cured meat – but so much more was packed into that old storefront. Another case was filled with *gastronomia*, prepared foods for sale. Fresh produce sat in bins in front of the refrigerated display cases, and beside the checkout counter was a small freezer with gelato. A shelf behind the coolers held some basic canned goods, but also specialty canned goods and jars of olives and oils from Italian and Sicilian importers, dried fish, and boxes of different pastas for a community that mostly knew two – spaghetti and macaroni. There were also bags of rice, and tins of unsalted butter. By the time the store opened, baskets of fresh bread were out on display too. Hanging above the counters, still more cheeses and salamis and gourds and baskets on display to accompany those in the windows. Behind the counter, impeccable wood and Formica counters awaited customer orders, knives gleaming in their holsters beside the old meat slicer. Under the cash register, to the right, a pistol rested in a holster screwed to the cabinet side.

The parking lot in front of the store stretched across the side of the lot, facing the Esso station. A single floodlight stood sentinel over the parking lot at night.

It had once been a neighborhood grocery, stocking all of the basic needs of rural people who bought only those things they could not grow or raise themselves. But, the family that started it, the Kesslers, they came from northern Italy, and they brought the family recipes. Soon, they were selling prepared dishes, and serving dinner one night a week. Then, the demand for food became greater than the demand for groceries. By the time the Key Market had opened in town in the early 1960s, Kessler's Grocery had become Trattoria de Vigna. Now, the Trattoria served lunch every Monday through Saturday– sandwiches, cold pastas – but dinner was served Thursday through Saturday, good hot Italian food, family style, or in big dishes to go.

The county was dry, and the Trattoria couldn't sell liquor over the counter. Locals "kept" wine there and starting back in the '50s, old man Kessler would bring out "your" wine in a carafe and let you know when your stock was getting low. Then he'd replenish it on his trips into wicked, wet Louisville. Even though it was really only a restaurant now, it had remained a touch point in Vintners Landing. People would stop in, headed into Carritherston or Frankfort, for a coffee. Some locals would make their lunch there, though most people took carryout.

And, because you stopped there, you could not help but notice the place and the people who ran it, who lived their lives on display. The show was tragic and entertaining, in a voyeuristic way. Part of the entertainment in the little restaurant was the emotional play among Danny's family. His grandmother, Donatella Kessler – just "Mama" to the family, was a tough old woman who could be affectionate toward you at one turn, stern and unyielding at another. She expected perfection and compliance, and she was domineering in her opinions and evaluations, which had not changed for most of the century. She was more nearly German than Italian in every respect except her cooking, which had been served up at the location since the 1930s when she and her late husband had come to town from Florida and opened the store.

Donatella's daughter, Angina, had bristled under the discipline and expectations of her domineering mother. She was an educated woman with a professional career (interior design), and she fancied big cars, money, tall men, and the pretensions of style and wealth. Married and divorced several times, she was an alcoholic with children by three men.

To cross them was to earn their enmity. For years Danny's grandmother had quit speaking to my grandfather and refused his business. Papaw – Marion Dixon – was a police officer, the day watch commander of post 12 of the Kentucky State Police. He was also a "mechanic," the man who rich men called to fix their problems and who poor people called to get a little justice where the law didn't quite apply.

He also had friends who would ask for a favor, or a favor too many, when they got crossways with the law. The way my cigarette-smoking, Episcopalian grandmother always told the story, she and Papaw would be asleep in bed in the middle of the night on any weekend when, invariably, the phone would ring. Usually this meant there had either been a bad wreck on the National Highway and they needed

Papaw and his color camera, or that a friend needed something fixed.

It was usually Dauby Nickles, the desk sergeant at the Brownsboro precinct of the Jefferson County Police Department, down in Louisville, who had the unfortunate duty of waking up Papaw. The phone would ring, and Papaw would answer it. If he sat up in bed, my grandmother would stumble to the kitchen and make coffee, because she knew ol' Merry was up for the day. Then she'd return to bed, and try to ignore the telephone and Papaw's conversations with the station.

"Marion? Merry?" Papaw had to be a tough guy with that name. "Hi. It's Dauby. Look, I've got this young gal down here, drunk off her ass, hit a phone booth on Lyndon Lane. Says she's a friend of yours."

Papaw would slowly come to life. "Who is it?"

"License says Angina Kessler. You know her?"

"Neighbor's daughter."

"She can pay the damage. Want me to cut her loose? Her brother is here too."

"Yeah, yeah. I'll take care of it. 'Night."

Once Angina went to the well, she couldn't quit. Every month or two she'd get busted, Papaw would get a call, and he'd get her cut loose. Then word started getting around that Papaw and Angina had a thing going on the side and that was why he was getting her out of trouble. It wasn't true, but it got back to my grandmother. She told old Merry to do something about it. So, the next time the phone rang at three on a Saturday morning, Papaw picked it up.

"Hello."

"Sergeant Dixon? Merry? Sorry to wake you up. Dave Barker at the Brownsboro Precinct."

"Uh-huh."

"I've got this drunk woman stopped on U.S. 22, says she knows you and we can't arrest her. We stopped her, weaving all over the highway, followed her coming from down by the river. She's hostile as hell, says she knows you and we can't arrest her. What should I do with her, Merry?"

"What's her name?"

"Angina Kessler."

Old Merry lay there for about ten seconds, and then said unambiguously, "Throw her drunken ass in the jail for the night and don't ever call me again when you pick her up." Then he took the receiver off the hook, put it in the drawer of the nightstand, turned back over and pulled grandmother close, and went back to sleep.

Up the road, retribution awaited Merry Dixon. Old Mrs. Kessler took it out on Merry with every customer who came in. She refused him business. They found a new place to eat and drink on Thursday nights. Angina needed to make new friends in the police department, because old Merry was through bailing her out of trouble.

Then there was Danny's brother, Salvatore. Sal was twenty years older than Danny. His entire life was dedicated to the Trattoria. The prospect of leaving to cook in New York was ended by his family in 1978. His mother had divorced, and was returning home to the store with her newest son, a little brother he loved but barely knew. Salvatore was needed to run the restaurant and take care of the family. His twin sister, Lenore, had married and moved away years ago.

Salvatore Lichten's life was entirely dedicated to the restaurant. The store opened every day at ten to do business with the local women who wanted to make Italian groceries, or who needed some catered food for the church social or the workaday lunch. The local women, they liked Sal – he was lean, and polite, and he served their needs. Every morning he rose, dressed in a starched shirt and a pair of khaki slacks, and swept up the porch and washed the windows to the Trattoria. Fresh meat delivery came at seven-thirty. Fresh produce was in the bins, stock was reordered and rotated.

In the summer, time was dedicated to picking fresh produce for sale from the gardens out back, sometimes being helped by a couple of the old black sharecroppers who also worked the tobacco and the grapes when they came in. The rest of the year, he'd drive the family's old white step-side pickup truck to the farmer's market in Carritherston to get what fresh produce they had not grown in their own gardens. On Thursdays he would drive into Frankfort and go to the liquor distributor to fill his customers' wine orders, and also stocked the whiskey and vodka that he sold under the counter without a liquor license.

At ten o'clock, the heavy wooden door was pulled open, leaving only a storm door with a cowbell ringer to hold out the elements. Then, he would start cutting meat for the morning shoppers, grinding coffee for the percolator, and would wait on customers headed from the country to the city, or chat with those who bought their cold cuts and swapped some gossip as they passed through. Dinner was a quick sandwich every day at eleven, supper every day at six when the last of the customers had passed through and the front door had been closed and locked. On Thursday, Friday, and Saturday nights, when they stayed open until eleven, he'd eat early before serving real Italian food to a small but loyal clientele that came in from Carritherston, Shelbyville, Eminence, and sometimes Frankfort.

At the end of the day, Salvatore went back out to the parking lot and swept the mess from the day's business. The shelves were checked and restocked, tables were stripped and cleaned and tablecloths were washed, the chairs turned up, the floor swept and mopped, and the front door of the store was locked and braced. Then he would take twenty minutes to count the till and lock the money in the safe in his grandmother's kitchen, and bring her the books to review. Bedtime was at ten most days, midnight on the nights they stayed open late. The day soon started again.

No business was done on Sundays, which were spent at the Salt Lick Baptist Church.

Salvatore wasn't a big man, maybe five-foot-ten, but he had a head full of wavy black hair, always closely clipped and groomed into place, and his big perfect white teeth shone in the manner of a salesman, which he was. As the years passed, his appearance changed some. He had some worry lines, but only a few grey hairs appeared, and he looked as fit at forty or fifty as he did at twenty. His entire life, he rose from bed, shaved, dressed, and did the same exact thing in the same exact way, and it seemed that as long as he did that, he wouldn't die. Salvatore didn't show any external scars, but they were there, quietly cut by a life where opportunity slowly flowed away. But he loved his restaurant and he loved his customers.

But he had no control, either over the business or over his life. As long as his Donatella lived and was active, she would control the business and make all of the decisions. His charge was to make it work, because family is far cheaper labor for so many reasons. And, he was a better cook.

Now, mind, he had his outlets. He loosed himself enough from his mother and grandmother to spend Monday evenings at a bar in Frankfort. Salvatore enjoyed his small charms. He was pleasant, and he had picked up some wit and charm from his mother. He also avoided her alcoholism, which had rendered her emotionally nonfunctional. Salvatore would only drink wine, and usually only with a meal, but sometimes he'd have two carefully measured glasses and talk to the ladies on their after-work nights out, or chat with the hookers who trolled for business in Frankfort. He was a good dancer. But he had no regular girlfriend or dated as far as any of us knew. But none of us knew everything.

When he had a girlfriend, there was only so far he could take the relationship. Living in a big family, with a home behind the family business left little privacy. Now, the family's home was spacious. A large parlor looked toward the house next door. As you topped the half-stairwell coming up from the back of the Trattoria, there was a side hall. The first bedroom off the hallway was his grandmother's, the second room was the parlor, the third room his mother's, the fourth Danny's, and the last room was Salvatore's. If he brought a woman home, he could not have been able to get her past "Mama" and Miss Angina, let alone survive the explanations that accompanied that effort. Most nights, he couldn't go somewhere else because he had to take care of the restaurant, or whatever else might happen during the night that frightened the old lady or his drunken mother.

Chapter 3

OUR FARM WAS OUT ON OLD BARD'S TOWN ROAD, which dead-ended into Grapevine Road, which ran through Vintners Landing. Danny and I, we made friends on the school bus at age six. Living out in the country, it was a long ride to school, almost an hour along a route that ran about twenty miles. That left a lot of time every morning and afternoon for the kids at the end of the route to get to know each other, and we were among the last stops on a road that winded out to the reaches of Cherokee County.

Danny had a quick wit. As a child he had been popular. He had wild grey-blue eyes and long yellow hair, and a devious sense of humor. He loved to have an audience, reveling in the center of attention. In the tacky, guttural world of little boys, he was a boy's boy. As Danny grew up, he developed two sides to his personality. He was respectful and mannered toward adults, insolent and brash to other kids who didn't follow his lead. And, as a consequence, he thought he could fool everyone. He turned into a liar who abused the loyalty and friendship of those around him.

He was aggressive, or passive aggressive, depending on the situation and with whom he was dealing. He loved to win, and, when we were kids, he was willing to try. But, if the breaks went against him he'd always find a way to avoid losing face, whether it was "accidentally" bumping a game board to disrupt the pieces or tripping a ball carrier that he couldn't tackle. He had quick speed to break away with a football, but if you gave him a good hit or even managed a shoestring tackle, he'd cry foul. No failure was ever his fault.

Danny had to win, but he wouldn't risk losing to win. Whenever I would think back to that time, what struck me is the shame of his lost talent. Danny could have been a good athlete, maybe even a leader. Possessed of quick hands and fast feet, he would have made a great receiver or soccer forward. He was speedy and sure-footed on the sand lot, but he wasn't willing to put on the pads and trade blows with the really good guys. He had animal intelligence, but his temper – and later his addictions – clouded his judgment. He couldn't work with authority or stand to be bested by others.

A lot of Salvatore's time was spent trying to fill the paternal role to a younger brother who had respect for almost nothing, including Sal. Their confrontations centered on things that Danny took for granted and which Salvatore provided. Sal was disciplined, giving, and responsible. Danny was self-absorbed, quick, and irresponsible.

As we approached adolescence, Danny started to alternate between reckless and mischievous. We'd go to stores in Louisville with Sal, on errands, and Danny would shop-lift. We'd be at the liquor distributor, and he'd try to get into the till, or he'd pull the fire alarm so he could steal a bottle. Then he and Salvatore would blow up in an argument; no one spoke on the long drives back to the Trattoria.

Salvatore paid the damages. Danny ducked any accountability. That was the pattern, Danny testing the limits of authority and trying to find power, then inevitably, crashing into something because his adrenaline would overtake his sense. And always, always, Salvatore was trying to reel him back in and try to keep Danny from landing in real trouble. No matter what happened, there was Sal to disapprove and bail him out.

I spent a lot of time in the back of cars and pickup trucks with Danny's family, listening to people not talk to each other. Those silences can tell you a lot, if you know how to listen. The storm would always break after I had gone home.

The side of Danny that made me uncomfortable was his racism. Now, in the South back then, you couldn't help but find racism, though the strain weakened from generation to generation. Danny embraced the smallness of large racism. He was quietly imbrued with a belief in white supremacy. He, however, managed to take it to a new low, by systematically prejudging every black man he met as his inferior. It was a common trait among the older men in the country, but it was something the next generation was supposed to move past. Danny reveled in the liquid taste of the words of white supremacy, in love with the notion that white skin made good kin. We didn't know to call him a skin head at the time, but he was turning into one, before our eyes.

I am not sure that the racism was entirely a product of indoctrination. His was a family of polite southerners who had to do business. In polite white society in the 1980s, you might believe these things but you didn't say these things. You didn't have to. The strict and emotionally confusing environment he was raised in, in a life where he had no control, no authority of his own, race gave him station. But, lots of things happen behind closed doors, and the hate and anger and abuse of his life had to come from somewhere.

Danny was weak in his desire to be strong. He wanted power but had neither the discipline nor the creed necessary to pay the price for power.

Instead, he became an obvious cheater. Looking back on it now, he spent time with younger kids because he knew he could win, and he knew he could capture the attention of them without as much effort. Maybe that's why he didn't really try in school, why he didn't compete. The differences in age and ability fell away; he couldn't keep up with his class and peers in a fair match-up. It was easier for him to be a smart-ass and a cheater than to hone himself on the discipline and skills of others. Eventually it was easier to hide at the bottom of a bong.

Then there were the drugs. Lots of us experimented with pot – it was cheap, it was everywhere, and it was not too strong. He got there first, and he got there worst. At thirteen, he was deep into marijuana use. He was headed for hash and coke by fifteen. I don't know if he ever went for the rock or the free-basing, but it wouldn't have surprised me.

All the crap he was running through his system, he couldn't really control it any more than he could control his envies. By the time he was seventeen, he was a year behind in school, having been held back. Drugs took over a large part of his life, and he became more and more isolated as his friends fell away one by one. He was on the quick ride to the fringe, not because of the drugs but because he couldn't handle them, couldn't handle anything. By the time I was in high school Danny had no tools other than anger and envy.

By 1990, he dropped out of school and took a GED. With the signature of his mother on the papers, Danny enlisted in the National Guard. She hoped the discipline and order would straighten him out. Danny just wanted to go kill someone.

Boot camp in Texas took some of the brash edge off of him, and monthly drill gave Danny some structure and responsibility. He made private first class, and worked in the Trattoria. He had a marksman's cross. He also became increasingly withdrawn the further he got from drill weekend. His mother, who had yet again moved back home, once more moved out leaving Danny behind as she again sought love from men who could only hurt her. Danny retreated into the small, private world of his apartment behind the warehouse, doing his drugs, and spouting rhetoric for grand plans of martial glory. What I only learned later was that he'd fallen in with some skinheads in the Guard. Within a few months he'd be out of the Guard, given a general discharge as a disciplinary case. His family never knew.

He slowly disappeared from my life. By then I had finally cracked the code on getting along in high school – as a former girlfriend told me once, swans blossom at different times in life. I started chasing girls and planning my escape to sun, beaches, and a college education. I didn't have time to find Danny, lost in his world.

Chapter 4

WITH DANNY AND HIS FAMILY, there was always trouble, always an argument, always a storm. Arguments over how to run the kitchen, fights over whether the Trattoria and its stocks of food were "too ethnic," fights over displays in the *norcineria* and *gatronomia*, disagreements over presentation at the tables, fights about family matters, all the arguments in the Trattoria raged in front of a confused, amused clientele.

Trouble came from many directions in the family. There was the collision of adolescent independence with the hierarchy of the old woman, disputes over Danny's lack of judgment and Sal's lack of authority. Trouble usually arises from bad judgment or a lack of respect. But, as is often the case, for a man trouble is usually in the form of a woman or money, and the biggest storm in that house involved a woman, a young woman. I always thought that Salvatore's troubles, and Danny's, started when Lana Rae Barnes came around.

Lana Rae was pretty enough. Not beautiful, and not really memorable, but definitely attractive enough to a boy who cared to look. My memory of her is pale, almost a reflection of her inherent lightness, almost white-blond hair and her fair skin that was dotted with just a few freckles. She was shy, prone to keep to herself.

The Barnes family rented the farmhouse on the old Gables horse farm, between our place and the intersection with Grapevine Road. Mr. Barnes was a farm hand and a construction worker, who split his time between cropping for the tobacco farmers and working roofing jobs around the county. A large man, his father had run-in with my grandfather years earlier when the old man would beat on his wife and kids. Papaw had laid him out good, and that was the end of the beatings in that family. Still, something never seemed quite right. We rarely saw Lana's momma, and her older sister, Jenny, had developed both her body and her habits toward the boys rather early. She was a favorite of the boys on the bus, and she reveled in their juvenile attentions. Jenny had a spark, and she knew that men wanted her attention. Jenny's smile and body shone so bright as to blind others to the existence of her sister.

Lana Rae walked through life, a pale blond girl who always seemed to be in the shadows.

The one person who always noticed Lana was Salvatore. He flirted with the girls who came into the Trattoria, especially the high school girls. No one ever knew if he was kidding or serious, but for a single man who lived at home in a small town, such acts sometimes sent the wrong idea to some of the mothers in town. But, they liked Salvatore and his smile, so they'd look past it.

Salvatore may not have attracted the notice of a lot of women, but he noticed Lana and she noticed him. That summer, 1988, my cousin Doug and I would ride our bikes up and down the old country roads, and we'd see Lana walking along the old one-lane road up to the main highway, a pair of Levi's rolled up to her knees and her hair pulled back in a pony tail. After we went fishing in the Fork, down below the old Landing, we'd stop up at the Esso for a Dr. Pepper, and there she'd be, across the parking lot, standing beside Sal while he restocked the produce, or unpacked the wine from the liquor store. Some way or the other, every day in the summer, you'd find her up there once a day, hanging out by the Trattoria and laughing and kidding with old Salvatore.

She never really laughed like that otherwise, at least not around the rest of us. Come fall, when school started, she'd get on the bus with her sister, and just sit real quiet by herself in the dark for the thirteen-mile ride to Carritherston. Or, on the weekends, when we would all sneak out and go camping in the woods or skinny-dipping in the sinkhole back in the woods off Hyatt's Store Road, she just hung back while her sister took all the attention. Salvatore was the only person who made Lana Rae light up, but you'd never know it unless you came around to see it.

Mama saw. Donatella Kessler carried authority and saw with clarity, and then combined it with a vindictive nature wrapped in her faith. She was right, she knew it, and those who did not see things her way were going to Hell, or were going to catch Hell. She was loving in her attentions to others' children, yet brutal in her assertion of authority over her own. And may the Lord help you if you crossed her or one of her own. To this day, when I hear a little child speak about her "*Mama*," I expect to hear that ancient old woman start yelling.

She was born into a middle-class mercantile family. They had come to America from northern Italy before World War I, Swiss Calvinists who left a Catholic nation, and they made good. To step into her Trattoria or her home was to be confronted with a world organized entirely around her tastes, preferences, and values. She was a devout Baptist, but often seemed to lack even the most basic Christian charity. She drove her children to great distances or to drink, and her grandsons were trapped in her domain, indentured to run the Trattoria while she presided.

She had probably once been an attractive woman; her progeny had a quality about them, a naturally attractive quality, though it was captured in lives born to sadness and an inherent perception of self-inadequacy, a bunch of caramel apples with soured, rotten cores.

The fields behind the Trattoria and the Esso Station were our summer playgrounds. When we were little, all us kids from the neighborhood played cowboys and Indians and war and football and all those other things that boys do. Sometimes we fished in the pond where Mr. Henschel watered his cattle, catching little yellowbellies or crappie and then pan-frying them over a campfire. When we got a little older, we raced motor bikes and cut across the back fields of the neighboring farms, learning the lay of the land, smoking cigarettes we stole from our parents or maybe sneaking out a couple of beers to split under the train trestle. A lot of days we played football in the fallow field between the tobacco fields across the railroad tracks, two passes for first down, and sodas and gelato on the porch of the Trattoria afterwards. All of us kids had to leave by five, unless you were staying for supper. Most of us never did, except for Doug and me. The old woman liked us, despite our grandparents.

Probably once a week in the summer we would eat supper with Danny and the rest of his family, usually on Wednesday. They always ate in the back of the Trattoria, in the kitchen, always at five o'clock, in order to finish in time for the after-work traffic or to get ready for the six o'clock dinner service on the weekends. Only paying customers ate out front.

One day, after a long day of hunting, playing football and sneaking beers in the backfields, Danny and Doug and I washed up and came into the kitchen for supper. We had bagged some rabbits that morning. Mama had prepared the hares in the *Veneto* style of northern Italy, along with *asparagi di bassano*, boiled eggs, and rice. Mama was in a mood, Miss Angina was stoned on painkillers, and Salvatore was working the counter.

"That boy, he doesn't have a bit of sense about him. Not a bit of sense." Mama Kessler intoned as she sat plates and silver before us. "Why can't he see the trouble he'll get in? Why can't he see? She's fifteen!"

Miss Angina sat at the end of the table, saying nothing.

"Well? Are you going to talk to him? Or shall I? He has no business –"

"Mother! Please. These boys are in from playing and they're hungry and thirsty. I'm sure they don't want to hear about this. It is not the time."

We stood to the side at the sink, acting as invisible as possible for three teenage boys.

Mama glared back at her daughter. "That may be," she turned her gaze on Doug and I, looking down over her little reading glasses. "Hayden, Dougie, maybe you'd best run on home after supper so that your folks don't worry. Danny, maybe you better see them back home too. Here –" she placed the serving dishes on the table, "someone ask the blessing and you go ahead and eat. We'll have ours in a bit. Danny, call before you leave to come home."

"Yes Mama."

Then the old woman walked out of the kitchen, up the stairs to the apartment above the store. I knocked out a quick "thank you oh Lord for Thy gifts we are about to receive" and crossed myself real quick in an act of Catholic defiance in a Baptist home. We gobbled down the rabbit and rice. Danny didn't say a word, but just seethed while he ate his dinner and stared across the table at his mother. She was either drunk or stoned. We finished our supper, and as we placed our dishes in the sink, Doug grabbed me by the arm and whispered "we better get on home." Out front of the Trattoria, Angina was attempting to see to a customer buying cold cuts.

Danny walked to the back of the storehouse and shouted "Mama! We're going up the road to Hayden's now." We headed out the back, through the storeroom and around the back of the store. As we came around the front, I glanced to my right and saw Salvatore walking around the back of the store, with old Mama Kessler hot on his heels, lecturing to the back of his head.

We tried to make out what she was saying, but the wind carried the words the other way. We got on our bikes and headed out the Grapevine Road.

The one time I was truly scared around Danny was that same summer after my fifteenth birthday, the summer Lana Rae started coming around.

At the end of May, a bunch of us went camping down by the turn in the railroad tracks headed for the river, to celebrate the end of the school year. That night, we ranged all over the countryside, getting soaked in the rain, drinking beer and smoking dope in the tents, and trying to cook over a Sterno can that wouldn't stay lit. At about midnight, a bunch of us trudged through the fields to get some bacon and burger we had left in the ice chest outside the Trattoria. After we got there, Salvatore insisted we stay, because the storm was growing worse. We made camp in the storage room and stayed up late playing poker and telling lies about girls we hadn't had.

The next morning, a Friday morning, we woke up and had breakfast. Salvatore took a call. It was Miss Angina. She had remarried that previous Christmas and moved to Cincinnati. Now, she had subsequently decided she was leaving her latest husband to return home. Danny and Salvatore had to go across the Ohio and pack her stuff up to move her back home. I called the house and told my parents I was spending the day at Danny's, and helping them move Angina back home.

We picked up a truck in Covington and went to the apartment Angina rented with her husband near the University of Cincinnati. It took the morning to do the packing. By lunch we had the truck loaded and the back of Angina's Mercedes stuffed with her other things. We were in a hurry, because it turned out that Angina had not informed her soon-to-be ex-husband Garth that she was leaving him, and she wanted to get out before he came home. Garth tended towards being obnoxious, drunk, and violent – a pattern for her with men.

The drive back was emotional. Salvatore took the truck, and Danny drove Angina's big black German car the ninety miles back from Cincinnati to Vintners Landing. She hardly said anything, just huffed and cried the whole way back, only taking the time to critique Danny's driving and to mutter under her breathe about Garth. I sat in the back of the Mercedes, holding a lamp and trying to be as small as possible, listening carefully to the silence.

After we got back to the store, we had a late lunch and then unloaded the truck into the rooms that Danny once again shared with his mother. Salvatore and Angina and the old lady argued for most of the afternoon, as Angina broke down and Salvatore tried to keep peace. Danny and I tried to keep out of the way by unloading the truck. The coming and going of customers watched the show, which needed to end soon if Salvatore and Mama were to be ready for the Friday night dine-out crowd. I couldn't head home until my parents got off work – I'd forgotten my keys.

Danny and I had just finished unloading the last of the things from the car. We were about to take the truck to the U-Haul place in Carritherston, when Garth's truck rolled into the parking lot. I was back in Danny's room, and looked out the open door where Angina and Garth were yelling at each other. Danny tried to get between them. Garth shoved him down to the ground, hard, and tried to take after Angina.

Danny ran through the house, crying and angered, and grabbed his double-barreled shotgun from the gun rack in back. He didn't even hear me as I yelled at him to stop. He just headed out the storehouse door, past the old wheelbarrow planter. More voices and screaming started to come from the parking lot. A few customers came out of the Esso and from over by the bank, and saw Angina and Garth yelling profanities at each other. I fell to my knees, tears streaming from my eyes, praying for God to find some way to help this angered, dysfunctional family. It was the last time I balked at fear.

Then I heard the shotgun blast from out the storehouse door. Danny was standing on the loading dock in front of the store room, and had fired a shot into the air and was yelling at Garth "leave-my-momma-alone-or-I'll-kill-you-you-son-of-a-bitch!" I ran to front door. By then I had found my own composure, such that it was. As Danny went to level the shotgun at Garth, Salvatore came running out from the store and grabbed the shotgun away from Danny as I came up behind him and grabbed Danny from behind.

Sal looked into Danny's eyes. "Get in that house and don't come out until I tell you otherwise." Still holding him from behind, I dragged him away and Angina pushed us both toward the back door of the house.

Salvatore turned to Garth. His voice was angered, but also utterly controlled. "I already called the police. You'd best get going and don't come back. I may not be around to control that boy next time."

It was about five-thirty by then. A police cruiser pulled into the parking lot, responding to the call. It was my cousin Scotty, who was headed home after his shift and told dispatch he'd take the call. After he and Salvatore talked for a few minutes, Scotty didn't write up a report. Instead, he agreed to just tell dispatch it was a domestic disturbance call "that got a little out of hand," rather than the aggravated assault with a deadly weapon that it was. He dropped me off at the house, and told my folks he picked me up as I was walking home and offered me a lift. I never told my parents about anything that happened that day.

That summer my cousin Doug got his first car, an old Bronco. We spent a lot of time tinkering in the driveway trying to keep it running. He had just turned sixteen, and I was thinking that sixteen would never come.

We hadn't seen much of Jenny or Lana that year. They had moved away for a while to stay with their aunt, and then had come back in March. I recall it was just after when their daddy had left their momma. Jenny was back in the swing – she dropped out and was chasing men and drinks. Lana was back too, and while she had developed more, she was still as shy as before, hanging in the background, always sad.

I would be riding my bike up to the store or over to my grandparents, and I'd see Lana walking along the road. Or, she might be out front of the Trattoria, drinking a soda or eating some gelato. But I would never see Salvatore out there with her. Whenever Doug or I went in the store and Lana came in, either Mama or Miss Angina would work the counter, and Salvatore would stay back behind the counter, quiet and involved in preparing meals for the evening rush.

That was a rough summer all around. Danny had turned sixteen that winter, his mother came home that Spring, and Danny cost himself nearly all of his friends. One day, while cleaning his room, Danny's grandmother found his stash in the bathroom. Now, a lot of us were experimenting, but only Danny was into the serious stuff. He'd been the first, but when he got caught, he played himself the victim. The discovery of his stash led to a four-cornered argument between him, Mama, Miss Angina, and Salvatore. He said it wasn't his, claimed that he was holding it because some of the other guys had hid the stash in the house. The old woman called everyone's parents, and a real stink got raised at the Landing.

The only guys he didn't implicate were Doug and me. But, he had showed himself as a liar and a sellout. He'd lost all of his friends because he had no accountability, no creed. When you get caught, you stand as a man and you take responsibility. And, you cover for the rest of the guys. That's the code, that's the way it is. Danny broke the code.

That left Doug and me with our own choice. It is hard to manage friends who don't like each other or trust each other. It is especially hard to be a friend to someone who doesn't follow the code. I couldn't justify his behavior – he'd shown both of his faces to all of us – he'd sell most any of us out to save his own ass.

I'll give him this much – he covered for Doug, for me, but he sold out the other guys. But he was drifting away and I had new friends, better friends with money and dignity. He was smaller in my eyes. I had outgrown Danny, outgrown his small wit, and was spending more and more of my time with the suburban kids who lived near the Lagrange Country Club, wore the alligator shirts, and drove the new cars.

He had stability of place – he had a home and was financially and physically secure. His emotions were a mess, because he had no one he could really trust, no strong, caring man or woman to parent him. He found a home in the Guard, for a while, but it just opened the door to the darker side of his anger.

I had guilt for abandoning him. But, what could I do? When I found out he was into serious drugs, the dangerous shit, I talked to my parents. They didn't tell me to drop him, but my old man didn't have a lot of room to trust him. Dad knew he used people, so he just had one more reason to keep an eye on Danny.

Chapter 5

THE NIGHT DANNY WAS KILLED started like so many others at the restaurant.

Danny said he had come home from Guard drill a few days before; or, at least that's what he said. He was running around looking for a full-time job, so he said, and after being gone all day he had scurried back to his apartment to hide out and get stoned. The reality was he was out of the Guard, probably dealing, and using drill weekends as an excuse to act as a mule for a dealer.

Evidently, at five as usual, he came down to the Trattoria to have dinner. Dinner was uneventful, I guess. I stopped to get an espresso on the way home from the library in Carritherston, and Salvatore checked me out at the counter and asked if I wanted to stay for supper. I was meeting Mike, a friend from up in Oldham County, later that night to go to a basketball game. Cherokee County was playing defending state champion Fairdale High, and hoops is king in the Bluegrass. I begged off dinner and headed for Louisville with Mike.

No one was yelling, yet no one was talking either. The fight would not start until long after I had left.

I am not sure what the fight had been about, or what any of the fights had been about since he had returned from his last two-week drill. Danny had carried a dark cloud around him since he got back in September, an air of trouble that kept him distant from most people around him. He wasn't even a "bad boy" who attracted girls – he was just an awkward loser who fought wars in his mind and lit up every night. He hid behind the arrogance of his accomplishment: he was a soldier now, a marksman, and he would fight in great wars for honor. But even then, behind the bombast and ego, something empty and troubled remained.

None of us who knew him and abandoned him were in a position to know. Events would have speak for the torments of his mind.

Most evenings, after the store closed, he and another friend, Randy, would sit out back of the house. Randy would drink the quart beers Danny bought at the National Guard post exchange while Danny would sit and slowly get stoned. Even then, though, the drugs and the liquor didn't disperse the cloud around his soul. That night, Randy and Danny sat for a while, talking and drinking. Randy left, to go see his girlfriend in Peytona.

Danny went out for a while, to where I do not know; maybe to score some coke, maybe to see someone. He used to buy from the two hopheads renting the house across the tracks, but then the house burned the summer before, and they moved on. Anyhow, when he got home, at about ten, Salvatore was waiting to see him in his room. The way the newspaper reported it, Salvatore had found out that Danny wasn't in the Guard anymore, that he'd received a general discharge for some misconduct. They argued for a while, walking though the house into the storage room between the residence and the Trattoria. Then, as the argument grew heated, they headed into the kitchen of the restaurant and were arguing behind the meat case. Danny grabbed a carving knife and tried to stab Salvatore. Salvatore grabbed a cutting board and swung it up to block, catching the blade in the hard wood and then knocking Danny to the ground with a backhand. The crash of the toppled stores rang through the tiny building.

Mama and Miss Angina were awake, and rushed down and were standing in the kitchen door to the store room, screaming and crying as Salvatore wrestled Danny to the ground in the kitchen. As they scuffled, Danny's mother moved into the kitchen, screaming for her boys to stop. Danny landed a hard foot on Salvatore's foot, elbowed him in the ribs before shoving past his mother into the house. He fled to Sal's room in back, locking the doors behind him.

Angina stopped Salvatore from going after him. "He's got those guns in there! Just let him calm down. Jesus, please! Just let him rest a moment."

Salvatore, gasping gulps of air, stopped, his hands resting on his knees. "Mama!" He called to his grandmother, "Call the police. Now Mama! Now!"

Danny locked and braced the doors to the residence. There was just one other door and one window in the back room he was holed up in. The door he blocked with a bureau and the box spring to the bed. The window offered a full view of the parking lot and the Esso station beyond, and had no blind spots. He blocked the window, from four feet down, with the mattress to the bed. It is all written down in a police report.

It was about eleven when the sheriff arrived on the scene, with a half dozen cruisers – a third of the entire county force and over half of the deputies on duty at the time. The dull thrum of a state police helicopter cut through the night over the empty fields, and the spotlight periodically swept the edge of the tree lines. The deputies deployed their cars, two in back between the apartment and the old lady's dormant vegetable gardens, the rest out front between the Trattoria and the Esso station.

The sheriff, Arlo Lowery, arrived soon after along with two state police cruisers. The state police had sent an investigator, Jethro Swearingen, who lived in Carritherston and was a trained hostage negotiator. Lowery knew Swearingen, and let him take operational command of the situation. In the meantime, about a dozen neighbors had come out and were gathered across the railroad tracks, three hundred feet away on the nearest neighbor's porch, trying to figure out what all the commotion was about. Some had heard the argument, and then all had heard the sirens. The helicopter had awakened another. Still another had been listening on his police-scanner, and recognized the address. The new paramedic vehicle from the county hospital arrived on the scene as a precaution.

Down in the Trattoria, Salvatore sat at the kitchen table, explaining to Arlo Lowery how the commotion had started, including the fight and how Danny barricaded himself up in the apartment. His hands shook as he spoke. Miss Angina sat at the other end of the kitchen, still despondent as a volunteer paramedic tried to calm her down. The old lady, Mama, stood by the sink, drinking a cup of coffee and saying absolutely nothing.

"So the fight started 'bout ten?" asked the sheriff.

"No, no Arlo, the argument started at ten . . . The fight started at about eleven, I don't remember exactly when . . . Maybe ten minutes before we called you." Salvatore described the knife and the fight in the storeroom. "That's it."

"Is he armed?"

Angina interjected. "God, yes, and he knows how to shoot too. He's a soldier, a soldier." Her voice trailed off in a slurred mumble.

"Yes, he's got guns. There's, there's –" Salvatore paused, stilted in his thinking. "There's a shotgun, and a carbine. Wait. Damn! He's also got the pistol from behind the counter. He was going to clean it for me today."

The report of a gunshot echoed into the kitchen through the door. Outside, the deputies and state police officers stayed under cover as a shot rang out from the apartment window and shattered the blue flasher on the roof of one of the cruisers. Across the highway, the neighbors scattered behind the house. Four more shots rang out, and two bullets struck the brick front of the house across the street, another glancing off the windshield of a sheriff's department cruiser, and the last finding no mark. Officers reported over the radio that the situation had turned from volatile to potentially deadly. The two state police cars and a deputy were deployed to stop traffic in each direction on the highway. One was just up Highway 14 by a local garage and towing service. Another set up about 300 yards across the railroad tracks up Grapevine Road. The third went down Grapevine the other way by Kermit Brashear's Key Market.

Inside, everyone had fallen to the floor with the gunshots. Angina was screaming almost uncontrollably now, and Mama was now praying under her breath for God's intervention, which was strange behavior for a Calvinist. Salvatore started for the back door to the storeroom, only to be stopped by the detective. "Mr. Lichten, damn it, you can't do anything now except get yourself killed! Sit down, and help me help save your brother or he may very well end up dead."

One of the deputies ran inside the front door of the Trattoria from the parking lot. He worked his way over to

Arlo Lowery. "Sir, he's let out five shots. No one's been hit, but it's a rifle. Sounds like a thirty-thirty carbine."

Another two shots rang out, one striking the ice chest of the Esso.

Lowery looked around, and picked up his radio. "Jethro?"

"Swearingen here. Sheriff?"

"What's your take, Jethro? He's got at least three weapons and lots of ammunition. Is he coming out?"

Another gunshot sounded outside.

The radio crackled. "Sheriff, this is Swearingen. No, I don't think he's coming out. Want me to call the special weapons team from Frankfort? If he hits one of those Esso pumps, this will be a huge mess."

Danny fired another round.

The sheriff keyed the mike on his radio. "Make the call, agent."

How Danny had arrived at this point was unknown to us then and now. His present, the moment that he would be frozen in, was to be barricaded inside that little apartment. I can only assume, as he shot and loaded and shot and loaded, that the adrenaline had overtaken Danny's mind. It is easy to imagine the battle in his head, driven by adrenaline. He was in a different place, in the middle of one of the fantastic battles of his mind. Awash in the conflict of his family, he was taking control and pushing the battle to the enemies of his mind.

The paramedics took the old lady and Miss Angina out the front of the store, to the ambulance that was parked beside out front, away from the main parking and the gunfire. Salvatore went out the front of the store with Arlo and the other officer. They were sheltered from the gunfire by the building.

"Sal, we can try to talk him out. We tried once, but he yelled something we couldn't make out and started firing at the patrol cars. If you want to try, that'd be fine, but I'm not sure whether he hears us."

"Where?" Salvatore responded, masking anxiety in his voice.

The detective motioned to move over behind the middle car, the one parked in front of the garbage cans and the light post in the middle of the parking lot. They ran over to the middle car, crouching down. Half-a-dozen officers kept their guns trained on Danny's makeshift sniper nest.

It took seconds but seemed like minutes. Salvatore crouched down behind the car with his back to it. Arlo Lowery knelt beside him, looking forward through the car windows while he fumbled with the megaphone.

"Here," he motioned as he handed Salvatore the bullhorn, "press the button on the handle to speak. You don't have to shout, but don't mumble. And keep the bullhorn facing forward, but keep down. He may be your brother, but to him you're just a target right now."

Salvatore turned around, and edged to the front of the car hood, keeping low. He keyed the mike on the bullhorn. "Danny? Danny? This is Salvatore!"

There was nothing. No gunshots. No response.

"Danny? Look, Danny, you need to just take a minute and calm down! Catch your breath! No one has been hurt yet, and if you'll talk to the detective here no one will get hurt! Just calm down and listen and everything'll be alright!"

Another moment passed.

Salvatore put the bullhorn over the edge of the car hood. "Danny?"

A shot rang out. A deputy threw Salvatore to the ground, and fell on top of him. Another half dozen shots shattered the windshield of the police car.

"That's enough of this crap." Arlo mumbled to himself. He grabbed the wounded bullhorn. "This is Sheriff Lowery! If the suspect opens fire again, return fire. Do you hear me Danny? We will return your fire! Now toss out that gun and come out with your hands on your head so we can get you some help! This is your last warning!"

Two more shots, this time from the pistol, went wild. Seven deputies and officers returned fire at the window, shattering the glass and splintering the wood around the window frame.

It continued like this for another five minutes, Danny firing and the police returning his fire. On the other side of the store, Mama and Miss Angina sat in the back of the ambulance, as the gunfire raged on the other side of the house. Each new exchange started another round of hysterical sobbing.

Then, the gunfire stopped, first for a minute, then two. Five minutes. Danny tossed the pistol out the window. Another minute passed, and a shadow cast across the open front door.

"Come on out. Toss out your weapon and come out with your hands over your head."

Danny must have thought his feet were fleeter than bullets, his training superior to the police before him. He burst out of the door, screaming at the top of his lungs, firing rounds from the carbine. As he tried to duck for cover behind the old wheelbarrow planted in the lawn beside the storehouse dock, he squeezed off another burst at the deputies to the left.

He should have looked to his right. Deputy Tyler Bridges rose up from behind the car to the far right, and, taking aim, squeezed off three quick rounds. The first struck Danny in his right knee, shattering the kneecap and dropping him to the ground. The second round passed through his larynx, exiting out the backside of his neck. The third round, quickly following the second, shattered the right side of his face, exploding out the back of his head. Danny fell to the ground, motionless.

He wasn't dead, but he also wasn't long for the world. Arlo called for the paramedics, and they came rushing around the front of the store. Angina and Mama came rushing around too, and seeing Danny lying on the ground pooled in dark blood, fell to each other crying. Across the highway, the neighbors started to peak out from the windows. Jethro called dispatch for the status on the medivac helicopter from Louisville. The volunteer paramedics tried to staunch the flow of blood from Danny's wounds.

The medivac helicopter arrived within ten minutes. A call from one of the officers on the ground brought it down, and it quickly landed in the middle of the highway, spraying water as it settled on the wet pavement. The flight surgeon and the paramedics went to work on Danny as quickly as they could. They gathered him on a gurney and carried him to the chopper. But it was too late. The headshot had killed his brain, and the body would follow on the way to the hospital five air minutes away.

On the ground, Salvatore walked over to his grandmother and mother and tried to help console them. The deputies secured the crime scene, and Jethro started gathering evidence for the after-action report that was necessary when a cop kills a suspect. Arlo separated his deputies from each other. An internal affairs officer from Frankfort would arrive about an hour later to take their statements regarding the shooting, which was later ruled as justified. Deputy Tyler Bridges would receive a commendation for defending his fellow officers under fire. By three-thirty the last of the photographs had been taken of the scene, the last witness report had been recorded. Television didn't come – it was too far out and too late at night for them to respond in a timely fashion. Arlo Lowery drove Mama and Danny's mother to Baptist Hospital in Louisville to see their boy and to find a doctor who could calm Angina's nerves.

Salvatore stayed behind until the police finished their reports. Then, he locked the Trattoria and the house, and drove to the hospital to be with his dead brother.

Chapter 6

THEY LAID OUT DANNY'S BODY for viewing a day after the shooting.

The funeral home on Main Street in Carritherston was just up the road from the high school. That fall I was carpooling with Tony Meier and Bill Grantholm; I would pick up Bill, and then we would fetch Tony and head to school. That day I told them that after school we were going to stop by the funeral home to see Danny. They were not too eager. Danny had dated Bill's sister, and Danny had ratted out Tony's brothers on smoking weed. Still, someone we knew was dead, and we had to go, to pay respects to someone for whom we had all lost all respect. That's the way you did things, even if you feel absolutely no sense of loss.

The Whispering Pines funeral home was built right after World War I. A square red brick building, it possessed a particularly stuffy air befitting its purpose. We parked across the street and walked over.

None of the family was there, and no other visitors had come to view the body. As we walked into the viewing parlor, the rain of the previous several days had passed and the sun started to break through. A soft midday light illuminated the parlor.

At the end of the parlor, opposite the chairs and nearer the windows, a mahogany coffin sat, the lid open. As we walked up, we could see Danny laid out for viewing. He was dressed neat, in a Sunday suit he'd never worn. The morticians had reconstructed his face from where the bullet had exploded into his skull, killing him almost instantly 36 hours earlier. There was something strange and artificial about it, like a plastic recreation of what his face had been, not quite fake yet also not quite real.

Bill and Tony were uncomfortable with Danny's body and the mortuary. They pressed me to leave, and we did, undone by the idea that life could end so quickly.

Now we had all seen dead people before. But they had all been old, old relatives whom we had seen wither before they expired. Not a week before we had seen Danny active and alive, with no indication that his days were so very numbered. I can recall now something I said to my mother back then. "You know," I said to her the evening after Danny was interred in the ground, "I could never imagine Danny old. I can see myself old, and I can imagine others of my friends old, but I never saw him that way."

Danny's funeral was two days after David and Bill and I visited the funeral home. Friends and family attended, as did many of the neighbors and customers. We all tried to console the family and to avoid the obvious question of how his rage had emerged into such a violent confrontation. After the services, visitation was held at the Trattoria. It was a Saturday night, but there would be no wine or music.

Mama was in a strange humor given her loss. A child should precede no parent in death, let alone a grandparent, and this family had lost its youngest son. Her bony arms gave me a warm hug and she appreciated my attendance. "You know, Hayden, we didn't see you so much anymore. Try to come around." Then she turned to Randy, the neighbor boy who waited tables on the weekend nights and minded the counter in the afternoons, "You know, when I call, you'll have to be my Danny now."

Miss Angina was catatonic. I could not tell if she was drunk, or simply numb from prescription painkillers. It may have been both. So much of her life was a wreck. Her oldest daughter, Sal's twin Lenore, rarely came home from Mobile. Salvatore had been the rock of the family who did whatever he was asked, and was consequently the direct beneficiary of the abuse and scorn of his mother and grandmother. She never saw her youngest child, a daughter by her third husband who was two years younger than Danny. She went to boarding school in Switzerland and mainly stayed with her Navy captain father during school breaks. He'd seen to that in the divorce.

As for Salvatore, one wondered when the day would come that his facade of good humor would dissolve in the face of the constant demands put on him by the women in his life. But that day never came, and the scars of Salvatore's soul were quietly cut more deeply. That day, the only issue was that Angina's baby boy, the one whom she loved but had never cared for, her baby was dead with a bullet through his head and he was lying in a coffin with a plastic face, dressed like a toy soldier.

It was the first time someone I knew, my age, had died. And it was an awful feeling. But I couldn't dwell on it. Where I grew up, in the land of the covered-dish condolence, death was part of life. Funerals were part of life – we'd go to several every year, mainly for elderly family who had passed on. By the time I was sixteen, I had been a pallbearer three times for kin. People came and went. Danny had died in my life long before he had his head blown off.

This last part has always been hard for me. I went to the funeral. I had been his friend since I was six, and I had been his most consistent friend, I was probably the last one to give up on him. And the family didn't ask me to be one of his pallbearers. It really hurt, because they couldn't find a sixth person, had to scramble to find that last pallbearer. No one bothered to ask me. No one thought to ask me. It made me feel invisible, irrelevant, small, like I hadn't left any sort of impression in his life. It also left me feeling conflicted. I was angry with myself for feeling slighted. Selfishness is out of place at a time like that, so I drove that emotion deep, locked it away, and left it to decay. Funerals are about family; they are about closure, and celebration. This was someone I was close to, someone who I had lost as a friend even if he was dishonest and unreliable.

As I left that evening and drove my old Mustang through the woody turns toward the farm, I couldn't help but think that maybe, just maybe if that family had shown each other a little more love and patience, and a little more forgiveness, and a little less spite and deceit, then maybe Danny might not already be in a mahogany box.

I didn't know if Danny was going to Heaven or Hell. If he went to Heaven, it was because God sees the young as innocent and seeks the better angels of damaged souls.

Chapter 7

I DIDN'T COME AROUND SO MUCH AFTER THAT, though I'd drop in to check on Salvatore and Mama, or get an espresso and chat with Randy while he tended the Trattoria. Salvatore was taking more time to himself, trusting Randy with the register and even running the front on weekend nights while Mama or Angina cooked. Randy and I, we had chased girls together for a while, until my tastes turned away from the whores that he preferred. I wanted a trophy.

The next year seemed to blow by. I spent a lot of time with Mike and some of his suburban buddies. Mike knew how to find a better class of girl, so I followed his lead. He knew his math and wanted to engineer things, but he also played a mean bass guitar and that meant we spent a lot of time trying to get into blues clubs in Louisville. Then, late at night, we'd wind our way back through J-Town and Fisherville, down the old Taylorsville Road, or come from Lyndon and through Propsect and Eminence, ducking cops and talking about the places we could go.

Sometimes, we'd just head out in the country and park in the fields below my family's farm, down in the bottom by where the tobacco was planted. Three or four of us – Mike, Devon, Erick – sometimes more, we'd lie on our backs and stare at the stars in the sky on a windless summer night.

"Hayden?"

"Yeah Mike?"

"Why are you so damn dark these days?"

"Huh? I'm not dark."

"Yeah, Hay-Hay, you are dark." Devon was our preacher's kid. His girlfriend Heike was asleep already. "I mean, look dude, I don't know what's bugging you, but why don't you just go get laid and shake it off. C'mon, man. You can do it."

"That ain't it, Devon. Getting laid ain't his problem." Mike lit a cigarette and kept staring at the moonless sky. "The problem is that he thinks he can fix the world. Ain't that right, Hayden? You want to fix the whole damn world. You need to think a little smaller."

"Like what?" I didn't really need their microscope. Devon chimed in. "Like fixing yourself. Not sure what's got you so dark, but if nailing Heike ain't gonna fix it, then it must be a problem."

"Devon?"

"Yeah Hay?"

"Where in the New Testament does it say that banging the drunken girlfriend of the high priest's firstborn will lead to eternal happiness?"

"Hah!" Devon choked on his beer. "It's somewhere in the Book of Luke, I'd wager, right after where it talks about getting a camel through the eye of a needle! Man, if hitting that isn't like eternal bliss, I don't know what is. C'mon Hayman, you need to go hit that."

"Devon," it was Mike. "Change subjects. Since Nichole says that Heike says you're not getting in there anyway, leave Hay alone. You decide where to go yet, Hay?"

"Florida. I'm going to UF."

"Fucking Gainesville? Why?"

"Money, man. Scholarship. And Daytona's an hour away. I gotta get out of here. I love you guys, but I gotta see something different. You can both have Lexington. Still headed there?"

"Yep."

"Yeah."

"Hayden?"

"Yeah Devon?"

"Why are you so damned dark?"

"Because the dark is the best place to go to see the light, Devon."

Mike had fallen asleep. Devon was quiet. We stayed in the field until dawn, and I drove them home after breakfast.

Once I headed off to college, I wouldn't spend more than a week or two at a time back home. Danny had been dead for over a year, but the pallor of his death hung over his family. I kept up with Mike and Devon, and would see them if I came through Lexington. They were playing some frat parties in a band with my cousin Doug, so we'd hit the parties, go out for some late partying, and then I'd drift off back to Florida.

II. A Long Sleepless Wrestle

Chapter 8

THE SUMMER AFTER MY FRESHMAN YEAR OF COLLEGE, I came home, briefly, for a few of weeks. The old man put me to work on one of the job sites, and I eagerly took union wages and put together pocket money for the next year. We were doing a power plant job in Hanover, and I worked as a tradesman, doing spot welding or whatever gofer work came along. One day, on the way home, I dropped in at Kessler's Trattoria to get a cold Dr. Pepper. It was a hot day, and I was drenched in sweat and covered in dirt, and thirst overcame any latent hesitation.

Fate presents me to beautiful women when I am not at my best. This day, fate reached down to do so in a little Italian deli where one did not meet beautiful women. Salvatore was working at the meat counter. I grabbed a soda from the cooler, and when I turned to go to the counter, there was a beautiful woman behind the register. She was willowy and black-haired, with sculpted features, olive skin, and the longest legs I had ever seen on an actual woman, wearing a blue flannel shirt tucked into a perfectly fitted pair of Levis.

"Hayden," Salvatore said, "You remember Tara?"

Fresh from a job site, covered in dirt and grime, I'm making introductions to the finest woman I'd seen all year. I did not remember Tara, but now, at this point in this store covered in dirt from a job site, I certainly wanted to know Tara. She was Danny and Salvatore's half-sister, about my age and fresh in from Europe. Her father had been deployed to the Persian Gulf, and she was set to start college in the fall at Transylvania. He had reluctantly sent her back to the mainland to work in the Trattoria and maybe get to know her mother. What I didn't know at the time was that he had also sent her back to get her away from her partying friends around their house on Honolulu. Tara needed to be tamed, to find some responsibility that boarding school didn't instill – so she got her journey to the Trattoria instead.

For some reason she smiled at me, and the next day I stopped in again on the way home. She slipped off her apron and we took a walk around the building, toward the cool east side where the shade was good and the customers were far off.

"So when did you get here?" I asked.

"Last month. I remember your name, but you're not like I remember. You changed." She smiled, I blushed.

"We grow, we change. I was always with your brother. Hey, look!" I motioned over by the hummingbird feeder. Two little hummingbirds flittered around the sappy feeder, tasting the sugary water and then flying off in an instant, disappearing, quicker than the blink of an eye. "What do you think of that? So beautiful, so fragile, so quick!"

She grabbed my hand and smiled. "Ask me out."

"Will you go out with me?"

"Yes."

We went out two or three times that week. We fell into bed the first time we went out, after we snuck into a jazz club down on Louisville's Second Street. We were not in love, at all, though really good sex affects a young man's head in a similar fashion. She was a wild lover, passionate and aggressive, and her smell and her touch lingered on my mind long after I left to go back to school for summer session. We wrote a couple of times but didn't see each other again until after my fall term.

Later, when I was home for the holidays, I asked her why she had slept with me that first time, so suddenly and forcefully. She had taken control of me that first time, saying nothing but exerting all of her energy on me. Tara said, "I don't know. I was so lonely here, and you were so different and honest. I felt safe with you and needed you then, like that. I was so lonely, and you took that away." She didn't like Transylvania, and she was looking for other options.

It was not a happy holiday for her. Her father had come out from the islands, and the fighting between him and his ex-wife Angina had spilled into Tara's life too. She was trying to untangle me from her, and I was trying to untangle my lusts from my heart.

The time I saw her, we went out for New Year's, hitting the black clubs in Louisville's west end and then taking a room at the new Hyatt downtown. I was ungracious and drunken, and got in a fight in the hotel bar. Some guy was hitting on her (so I thought). He wasn't. But, I was prideful and couldn't admit the mistake. After I took her home the next day we never went out again, as much by a mutual understanding that I had behaved like an ass as anything else. It was not the last time I would lose a relationship for being a boor, though eventually the lesson took.

The next day I left for Florida, and I rarely came home afterwards. It had less to do with her than with the pull of other places and other faces. I glimpsed her once more, about a year later, when I was home for a wedding and out with Mike and Doug. Mike pointed her out to me, but I had moved on to other loves and other lusts, and didn't really want to go back to dealing with the sad craziness of her family. I could get laid elsewhere, I told myself, and turned the other way to avoid her.

I suppose I had not thought about how sad and hard her life was. It is hard to imagine that life is difficult for beautiful people, but it is. She had left a warm and hopeful place where she had lived on her own, to come to the gray skies and cold weather of the mainland, to live with her drunken mother who she didn't really know and a controlling grandmother. She was cooking and waiting tables in the Trattoria, and going to a college she didn't really want to attend. She disappeared into life and I lost track of her, though a couple of times I did look before I decided it was time to move on. I thought the world was too small in Vintners Landing.

Chapter 9

OTHER THAN THE BRIEF, INTENSE FLING with Tara, I had barely
made contact with anyone back home except family, and
even those ties were not strong enough to pull me back home
very often. What it was, I didn't understand – I still don't.
Perhaps someplace else would allow me to be someone else.
Why I wanted to be someone else I do not know. The mirror
wasn't providing answers when I looked into it. And, as I
found out, the horizon offered no answers either.

After four years in Gainesville I walked with a degree
in architectural history and a burning desire to tromp the
world shooting slides with my camera. The problem was that
no one was willing to subsidize my foray into gentlemanly
leisure, so I moved to Athens, Georgia, and took a position as
an assistant project manager with a small architectural firm.
I'd work all day. Then I'd go party most of the night, most
nights of the week. I had no sense of where I was headed.

One night, I was doing shots with some frat boys at UGA, in a
little joint called the Georgia Bar. I was supposed to meet
some people to watch REM play under a cover name over at
the Uptown Lounge, but word got out and the place was soon
packed with people. I couldn't find the people I was meeting,
so I slipped down the street to this other little joint.

"Damn. You sure can drink for a fucking Gator."
Fraternity boy number one observed, as he tried to catch the
bartender's attention to order another round.

"And you sure can spell for a Bulldog. Oof!" I was
drinking a lot back then, and the company consisted of
whoever was willing to go. "Hey, they got any fresh roasted
peanuts over there? Bartender!"

Fraternity boys number two and number three decided they couldn't wait for the bartender. When they went to serve themselves, the bouncer kindly asked us to leave. He being not open to negotiation, we decided to leave. That same stunt got the three frat rats tossed out of our next stop, the Odyssey Bar. I hung back, didn't get caught in the bouncers' sweep through the bar. Instead, I just lingered off at the back of the bar, watching football highlights on the TV.

An elbow in my back and a wet splash on my shoulder brought me back to earth. Annoyed, I turned ready to fight, and instead saw a bunch of coeds who had come in the latest wave of sorority girls. They had stormed the bar from the pool tables one of them got knocked into me by the wave of party girls.

"Oh! Oh! I am, like, so sorry about that. Hey, oh, I am so embarrassed. Are you okay? Oh shit, I baptized you didn't I?"

She was maybe five-three, wearing a sundress with her long dark hair pulled back in a ponytail. She had high cheeks and big green eyes.

"It's no problem," I muttered, trying to smile. I couldn't take my eyes off her face. "Momma said I'd find religion someday. I'm Hayden."

"Tracy. I've never seen you in here before tonight. What house are you in?"

"No house. I was with some jackasses who got thrown out of the Georgia Bar, and then they got tossed from here. I'm flying solo now."

She bought me a drink, and conned a towel and a t-shirt from the bartender and made me change in the middle of the bar. We tried to talk for a few more minutes over the noise of the crowd, but it seemed like all we were able to say was "what!?!" Tracy grabbed my head in both her hands, and yelled into my ear, "This pickup palace is too crowded. There's no live music! Let's get out of here! C'mon! There's some new band at the 40 Watt Club!"

She dragged me through the crowd to the front exit. We ducked out and turned right, making our way into downtown Athens on Clayton Street. The crowd was still spilling out of the Uptown, where Michael Stipe was going on about something political. When we got to the 40 Watt, I went to pay the cover, but the manager, Barrie, just waved Tracy in with a big smile.

Back then the 40 Watt was a tiny place. It was just an empty storefront with bare brick walls and a bare-bones bar. When we went in it was maybe two-thirds full. Hillbilly Frankenstein had just finished a set and the second act was setting up. Tracy and I got a couple of drinks and found a piece of wall near the stage.

"Guys, we got a treat for you tonight. These guys are out of Lexington Kentucky –" Boos and barks cut through the crowd. "– no, no, none of that! These boys can flat out play! They've got an album they just finished laying down yesterday in Atlanta, and they're making their Athens music scene debut! Guys, put them together for Fake Chipotle!"

Five guys in green t-shirts, green jeans, and mirrored shades came out on stage, and plugged in. They looked familiar. The sound caught on with the crowd, and pretty soon stage was a crush of dancing Bulldogs and alternative music scene locals. Tracy and I got into the crowd dancing, and worked our way near the stage. We danced the whole set of Fake Chipotle and also the next act, the Velcro Shoes. At about one AM they shut down the liquor, but the music kept going until two. We danced and laughed and didn't say a word, just taking in the music.

Finally, at two in the morning, we walked out front. "Hayden?"

"Yes Tracy?"

"Want to get something to eat? C'mon! I'm hungry. I know a place."

"It's two in the morning. What's open besides the truck stop and the Castleburger?"

"C'mon. I'm from here. I know a place."

She grabbed my hand again, and we just walked and bopped south from the 40 Watt, toward the police station. "Here it is."

"What, the police station?"

She slugged my arm. "No, you big silly! Over there!" She pointed to an old storefront across the street, with a deck on the front. "There!"

The sign over the window said 'Herbie's.' We wandered over to where a crowd of people was waiting in line.

"C'mon! We don't have to wait." Tracy pushed her way through the crowd with me in tow. When she got to the door she shoved her way in past the crowd by the cigarette machine and the cash register.

Inside, a pair of ancient black men in white aprons and paper hats worked two griddles. Three young waitresses hustled orders and flirted with drunken frat boys. And, in the middle of it all, a squat little bald guy with a cigar and a sweaty complexion held court, coordinated the kitchen, and made people laugh.

"Herbie! Hey Herbie!"

"TC! What are you doing little girl?" Herbie muscled his way through a crowd of drunken college kids and gave Tracy a big bear hug. "Your daddy know you're out this fuckin' late? And who is this here douche bag?"

"Be nice Herbie! I happen to like this here douche bag! Hayden, Herbie. And this–"she dramatically waved her hands around "–this is Open All Night! My People! Uncle Herbie, we need a table. And two big Denver omelets!"

"Right this way sweetheart. You and the douche bag can go right out on the deck and take that table by the rail. Ol' Herbie will come check on you in a minute." Herbie poked my gut. "Hey, douche bag, what'd the basketball say to the football at the hockey game?"

"I don't know."

"Let's get the puck out of here before someone slaps him around again." He laughed and shoved me through the door to the deck.

Tracy was making her way through the deck crowd. It seemed like everyone knew her, or knew of her. She was an infectious sprite who loved to play a crowd. She'd shriek with the girls and slug the guys in the arm and then kiss them on the cheek.

We finally made our table. "Damn. This place is different."

She sat down by me, and we both looked out toward the crowded deck. "Yeah, but it's a great idea. Herbie started it years ago to take advantage of the 'after hours' crowd. He opens at eleven and closes at five, and the cops make sure there's no trouble. They like him."

"Why?"

"He keeps the drunks off the street, gets people straight. Herbie is profane and rude, and he's also a prophylactic against drunk driving."

"Never thought of it that way. How'd you know the place?"

"I used to sneak up here in high school. Then, I worked here for a while when I was in college. I still take a shift now and then, but mainly I work at Allen's over in Normaltown, at least when I'm not painting."

"You're an artist?"

She filled me in. She had traveled a lot with her father and mother, and they had not let her have television at home. She loved to write, and paint. She loved oils, and she loved to paint slices of life of the night. She saw the world as a canvas, and danced until she knew what to paint, then painted until she needed to work. Her eyes sparkled as she talked. They were bright green, the pupils surrounded by darker green circles, like little halos. I swam in those perfect green circles. She talked and talked and talked, and I just sat there, getting lost in her stories and alone in the universe with her.

We talked until almost dawn, and then walked from downtown toward Prince Avenue. When we got to the old shotgun house, she turned around and looked at me. "That was fun, Hayden. I think I might like you. Want to come in."

I looked down at her, smiling. "Yeah, I do. But I won't."

She gave me a fake, hurt look with a little smile. "Why not?"

"Because I love you too much to ruin it. Sleep with you, now, would ruin it later."

"Smart answer, Hayden. Call me?"

"Absolutely."

She wrote her number on my hand with a marker. "Don't ever wash it off. But if you do, come in Allen's tomorrow night and I'll put it back. I go on at six, get off at two in the morning." Then she was gone, headed into the house and leaving me in the flat grey of the early morning.

I forgot where I left my car. But, I didn't have to be at work until noon, so I wandered back to my apartment on Spring Street and got four hours sleep.

But first I wrote her number down. Twice. And I didn't wash my hand.

The rest of the day was a fog. I came in at noon, and Curtis, the boss, had already taken off for lunch. I almost called Tracy, but decided to follow the old rule of 'wait a day' before I called her up. Instead, I plowed into the specs for a luxury dorm that Curtis was bidding to build near UGA. My job was going over the pricing from bids before we submitted.

Curtis came back in about 1:30, and then called me into his office. "How's the bid looking there, Rollin?"

"Fine sir. I ran all the numbers again and I also put them into that new spreadsheet program. Everything is checked and double-checked. I'll have the bid ready by tomorrow afternoon."

"Good stuff." The phone rang, and Curtis took the call. ""Yeah, yeah Ma. Yeah, I know. I tried to talk to her. S'okay. Yeah, me too. Bye."

The balance of the afternoon was finishing the draft of the bid proposal. At five, the rest of the office staff had knocked off for the day. I went back in Curtis's office and briefed him up again on the project. Then as we were finishing up, we heard a voice making its way through the empty office.

"Daddy! Daddy! I have got to tell you about this guy I met!"

"Back here, honey! You're grandma warned me about this. Who is it this time?"

The voice got to the door, and I turned in my chair to look. Tracy stopped for a second. Then she smiled, looked at me, looked at Curtis, and pointed. "Him, Daddy. Hi Hayden!"

Curtis leaned back in his chair, crossed his big arms, and just started laughing.

Chapter 10

WITHIN A YEAR TRACY AND I WERE MARRIED.

Curtis was generous. He took us into the business. He was doing tract developments outside of Lawrenceville, and, thanks to a housing boom on the northeast side of Atlanta, we were flush with business and making money faster than we could count it. I started a doctorate in landscape architecture at UGA, taking a course or two as I could.

I really wish I could have known Curtis better. Not too long after we got married, he was killed in a one-car wreck coming back from his lake house near Toccoa. He had started building luxury cabins up that way, and he was returning from a negotiation with a developer in the area when his car was run off the road. Tracy's mom had died years before, so she and her brother inherited the business.

We kept the company going for another two years, until a major developer bought out Tracy and Camp. She had enough money invested to live comfortably, so we went to try something different. I was tired of working on developments. I just wanted to work on my thesis and be surrounded by pretty things, old things with history and craftsmanship. Tracy was tired of Athens and just wanted to paint. She had always wanted to live in New Orleans, so we went down there and started looking for a place to renovate.

We found a place in a funky neighborhood called the Lower Garden District, between Magazine Street and the river, on Melpomene Street. The house was an old side-by-side shotgun double; we figured to open it up into a single. The neighborhood was about to rebound, we thought, and the house was a jewel in the rough. We bought it, and then ripped out everything from the floor joists to the rafters.

Four months after we started we had finished. Tracy was painting, hanging out around Jackson Square and scouting subjects in the coffee shops on Magazine Street. We'd hit the Maple Leaf and Tipitina's and dance all night, trying to find that perfect story for her to capture on canvas.

Not long after we finished the house, I knew I didn't want to go back to tract development. But, I was restless and stuck on the thesis. The restless edge overtook my conscience. I tried to follow my grandfather's career, and I went and joined the New Orleans police department.

The pay was lousy and half the force was corrupt, but I made it through the academy, and ended up working the mounted patrol. Our beat was mainly around the French Quarter, though they also sent us into some of the rougher neighborhoods to intimidate the gang-bangers, because a man on horse can control a crowd of a hundred, and the corner boys and street punks were scared to death of the horses. Six months later I was switched to work with the homicide squad, because I seemed to have a mind for detail and my precinct commander thought it was a good fit. Also, he thought I was onto one of his little side deals. As I later learned, he figured it was easier to transfer an honest cop than to kill one.

The detail they put me on collected crime scene information for forensics. Once in a while, they'd partner me with one of the homicide detectives when someone was on leave or sick. Tracy painted, working images in her mind from the stories I would tell of the impoverished underside of New Orleans.

The end for me on the police force came quick enough. Just two years on the force was enough to turn my gut, to consider getting out. One summer evening, just before I went on duty, Tracy and I went to Parasol's over on Constance and got a couple of sandwiches for lunch. She knew I was miserable.

"Hayden, honey, I can't stand seeing you like this. You're so dark and distant sometimes. You're not sleeping either."

"I know. I thought I'd do some good in this job, you know. But police work in New Orleans is hell, especially when you're on the homicide squad of a city that has four hundred homicides a year." I felt like I was ready to cry. I had seen enough.

She took my hand in hers. "Then quit. Quit tomorrow. Quit now."

"Tracy, it isn't that simple honey, and you know it. My Papaw spent thirty-three years on the county police department. He never slept and always worked."

"You ever wonder why?"

"I used to. But now I think I know why."

"Tell me, Hay. Tell me why. Then maybe you can sleep."

"It's the eyes. The images of the dead, the injured, and the tormented never leave you. And the glassy, soulless eyes of the killers and rapists and abusers stun you with their complete lack of compassion or remorse. Who can sleep when sleep brings you nothing but images of those eyes from Hell?"

"Honey, are you willing to listen to me?"

"Yep. Yes I am."

"You made a mistake. And now you think you have to live with it. But you don't. Just quit. Quit tomorrow. We don't need the money. What there is of it won't cover your therapy."

"Tracy, I'll think about it. Really, I will, honey. Look, I'm twelve-on, twelve-off on until Monday, and then I've got three days off. We'll talk when I get home."

She dropped me off at the precinct down on MLK Boulevard. We didn't get to talk that night. Instead, that night I caught a bullet in my right lung.

We were responding to a shooting in New Orleans' Central City, near the Melpomene project. A couple of gangs had dusted up over drug turf, and we came in to secure the crime scene – two guys dead, two wounded taken to Charity Hospital's trauma ward. As we were taking statements, some thirteen-year-old punk with an Uzi decided to take a shot at the guys we were interviewing at the crime scene. Two bullets caught me under the arm where my flak jacket didn't offer protection.

The next morning, sitting in Charity Hospital, I called my captain and quit. Policing New Orleans was hopeless. And there was sleep to be had.

I like sleep. Sleep gives you the chance to sort your mind, and a particularly good sleep helps you build your own reality. I wanted to sleep, I wanted to build. I found myself walking into a neighborhood church, where the preacher worked a lot with a local group that renovated abandoned houses. New Orleans had thousands of abandoned and dilapidated houses before Katrina struck, adding to the total. Back then, there were lots of working poor families that wanted to get out of public housing, but they were trapped in the cycle of poverty and dubious credit. The preacher started me out inspecting donated houses to see if they were fit for renovation.

Tracy was finding a niche for her art, which combined the stories of New Orleans' streets with a style resembling industrial realism. I was enjoying doing one house at a time for clients who didn't complain if the marble in the kitchen wasn't just the right shade of mauve. I finished the thesis, and taught a class at Tulane. We were not getting rich, but we had few obligations. Tracy's investments compounded and we lived a quiet life of art, barhopping, and charity. And, unlike when I was doing the police work, I could sleep at night.

One night, a Thursday, we were walking back home from dinner, it all seemed to come together. We were walking down Napoleon Avenue toward Saint Charles, coming from theis barbecued shrimp place that she liked. We usually avoided the place, but she wanted barbecue shrimp so there we were. The trolleys were running slow, and it was an unusually cool, dry night for February, so we decided to walk. Carnival was underway, and a parade had just made the turn on Napoleon at St. Charles.

The breeze picked up. She snuggled up against me. "Oh, one other thing I forgot to tell you. I want to go looking for a new house."

"A new house? What for?"

"Oh, I don't know. I like the one we have, but, it just isn't ... right for us."

"What do you mean, right? It is perfect. Just enough room, right near the restaurants we want. I mean, what's missing?"

"Well, there's no yard, and not enough room if we're going to have a baby."

I stopped walking. It had finally hit me. "A baby?"

"That's right." Those green eyes sparkled at me again. "I went by Doctor Crittenden's today and she said so. Think you're finally ready? Are the dark ghosts gone?"

There is a stunned, numbing feeling that accompanies pending fatherhood, a peculiar combination of joy, pride, and fear that emanates from somewhere between the brain and the heart, and which therefore gets stuck in the throat, preventing both speech and rational thought. I grabbed Tracy up and swept her around.

"Yeah, yeah, the ghosts are gone, or at least nicely distant. No dark ghosts or visits from the black dogs from now on."

She let me carry her for the better part of a block, curled up in my arms, a big stupid grin on my face.

When we got to the corner of Milan at St. Charles, the parade had finally completely made the turn. The crowd was now gathered ten deep all around, and the heart of the krewe caught up with us. All around us kids and drunks dived after beads and plastic doubloons and stuffed bears. Groups of young kids snaked in and out of the crowd, hanging together. The littlest kids were perched on benches on top of eight-foot stepladders, all the better to see the parade and not get crushed. The king of the parade's float was about to overtake us, with some drunken comedy actor sitting on the throne. The crowd surged close, because the king's throws are usually the best of the parade.

Behind us two gangs of local kids working through the crowd ran into each other. From the corner of my eye I could hear the yelling, but I wasn't sure what had happened. Then one of the mounted police, Jake, my old watch commander, turned and started to move in their direction.

Then I saw Tracy flinch at about the same time that I heard a dull popping sound. She fell onto me, and I instinctively turned and saw the crowd scattering as the two groups of local toughs shot away at each other. The sound hurt my ribs.

I dropped to the ground. All I could do was stay down as gunfire passed back and forth overhead. Most of the crowd scattered into the midst of the parade and away from the shooters. The half-dozen or so cops at the turn were still getting a handle on the location of the shots. Eight people were shot, injured or dead.

The shooters ran. The mounted police chased two of them down on the scene, and investigators later found two more of them. Around us, the crowd was gone, dispersed into the side streets. Sirens screamed, approaching from downtown.

I sat up on my knees, beside Tracy. She was dead, her body hanging limp in my arms, but she had an odd smile on her head and her eyes wide open. I closed her lids, laid her back on the ground, and just sat and stared until an officer who I knew approached me. I was thirty-one and alone. That was when I started sobbing, quietly. Not for Tracy, but for me. We never really cry for the dead.

Chapter 11

We buried Tracy back in Winder, outside of Athens, in her family cemetery. I couldn't go back to New Orleans, not right away. Family had come in from Kentucky, frinds from New Orleans, but they were just shadows, background figures to my loss.

A week after Tracy had been killed, two days after the funeral, friends and family were gone. I stayed in Georgia, and Tracy's brother Camp went with me to Toccoa, so I could spend a couple of days thinking things over. He knew I liked to talk to him, liked the way he listened.

"So Hayden, are you going back to New Orleans?"

"No," I muttered. "Not now. Not yet. That is not an option. The beauty of the city had come through Tracy's eyes, through Tracy's heart. The only way I can hold on to her is to hold onto the beauty of that splendid, decrepit place as she had seen it. I can't do that right now. All I'd see is death."

"What about Atlanta? Come back up here. We can do something. Just stay at the lake until you figure things out."

We talked more, but Atlanta wasn't an option. It was too expansive, too busy, and too invested with babbitry to suit my taste. I turned my options over and by dawn, sitting on the dock, a plan of action took place.

"Look, are you sure, Hayden? Looks like you're just running off again. Grief requires process, time. And support."

"No. I'm sure. I'm going for a walk. I've got a friend in New Orleans, realtor. She can sell the gallery and have the art shipped up here to store. I want to keep the house, just in case, but she can arrange a lease tenant. Can you manage affairs for me back here?"

"Like a trustee?"

"Basically, or a business agent."

"Sure. How will I find you?"

"i'll have email."

A week later, the paperwork was done. I grabbed a backpack, slipped on a pair of hiking boots, and headed up the Appalachian Trail.

I ended up in Vermont, still running from a ghost. It was a good place to knock around. I spent a little time working on a construction site, but by the end of summer a more substantial change of scenery was in order. I hitchhiked down to Boston, and boarded a flight for New York and grabbed the first international flight I saw, to Korea. Katrina hit New Orleans while I was in the flight, and my heart broke again.

For the rest of the year, I sat in on lectures in the architecture school at Seoul National University. Then, an email from an old friend from UGA caught up with me. He was on a Fulbright in Hungary, and he thought I'd enjoy joining the design clinic at their university. Korea wasn't turning out like I had hoped – Seoul is dirty and the Koreans like to argue too much. So, I hoped a Lufthansa flight to Munich and then caught a train to Budapest, to fill in for a year as a visiting professor at the Institute for Urban Design.

When I was in Burlington I had started sketching the elements around town, just to keep my head empty. When I got to Korea the first time, I started reading the trendy Asian design literature, and that set me to thinking about the basic concepts of form and utility and harmony in human space. It was in Hungary that the ideas started to come together.

So my time in Budapest was spent writing a book on architectural theory and urban growth, titled *An Organic*

Theory of Human Space. Friends in Seoul wanted me to come and spend some time walking them through the premise and implementation of my thesis. I declined. After over two years on the road since Tracy was killed, it was time to come back to the states and reestablish relationships in the family.

I booked a flight to Atlanta.

Chapter 12

Last April

WHEN I DECIDED TO COME HOME to the states, the first questions to be answered were what to do, and where to do it. The house in New Orleans was still there, dry and undamaged despite the hurricane. But New Orleans still hurt; Tracy's ghost would confront me at the turn of every corner in Uptown.

The decision was made for me the month before I left Budapest. Mike, my school friend from Lagrange, dropped me an email. He'd read *An Organic Theory of Human Space* when I'd sent it to him, and he in turn had handed it to a buddy of his who was dean of the Speed School of Engineering. They wanted me to come back to the city and visit about some opportunities back home. Mike said he had a business opportunity he would cut me in on, if I was willing to take the risk.

So, at the end of April, I packed up my apartment off the Gomb Utca, shipped the boxes ahead to my parents' place in Vintners Landing, and grabbed a cab to the airport and flew to London, and then on to Atlanta. Tracy's brother Camp had kept my old Mustang for me while I was abroad. We visited for a couple of days, talking football and missing his sister before I headed north on I-75.

When I got back home, Mike arranged for me to have lunch with the dean at the engineering school and the dean at the Urban and Public Affairs school. U of L doesn't actually do architecture, but they have a great urban planning program. And, the deans thought a series of lectures on the organic theory would be of some use to the engineers. So we worked out an arrangement for me to act as a visiting fellow – I'd come in a day or two a week, give a series of campus lectures, and help out some graduate students and design students. It wasn't fulltime work, but it gave me a professional home.

The real offer that got me home, though, was what Mike showed me as we walked from campus back to his Porsche. As we headed from the campus toward Saint James Court, Mike looked at me and said, "You know, this is a nice neighborhood. It used to be a center of arts and creativity in this city. Look at these houses. The university would like to clear them for campus expansion. What a waste." We stopped in front of an old brownstone. "Look at this place, Hayden. Victorian architecture, gorgeous turret, probably built about 1880. No one living in it right now. Electric and plumbing are not up to code. Uninhabitable."

I eyeballed the old house. "Structure looks solid enough. Foundation's probably good. Looks square enough."

"C'mon. Let's go in." Mike headed for the front door. It was open.

For the next hour we walked around the old brownstone, checking out the structural features, the original architectural elements, the wiring, admiring the leaded glass.

"Hayden, I think we can get all eight buildings. The guy who owns the three apartment houses agreed to sell at a reasonable price, good for the market. Of the five other houses, this one and one other are foreclosures that I picked up already, and the owners of the other three, I bet they'll sell. Two of them are not up to code and stand to be condemned."

"Back up. We?"

"Look, we've always talked about working together. I think this is the project. I read your book. Part of the organic theory has to do with the recycling of space in a manner that preserves the aesthetic while accommodating the need of the occupant – respecting history while accommodating the future, helping evolve a community while preserving its value. So what we do is we do an organic flip – work with recycled and reclaimed materials to reclaim the historic elements, incorporate new modern features that are consistent with the aesthetic of the house but which optimize the efficiency of the design. When we were in school you always said that wrought iron and old brick and wood floors would find a market. These houses fit the bill."

"Mike, what about the neighborhood? Saint James Court is over by the park, and those houses never come on the market. Campus is two blocks the other way, but the neighborhood is for crap all the way to the racetrack. And we're on the edge of it on this block. This is a five-block area that is hanging onto the edge of the edge of the campus and the edge of the edge of prosperity. If we renovate as single-family dwellings using organic theory, it'll take six months to flip each house, and they'll have to sell for a hefty price to justify the job. Can this neighborhood support steep prices?"

Mike smiled and laughed. "Hay-Hay, it's your lucky day. I know something no one else does, and it'll make these properties some of the hottest homes in town. The university is about to announce that the state is allowing them eminent domain to redevelop everything across the street all the way to the campus. Three city blocks. They're renovating some of the buildings for faculty campus housing, but most of it is getting cleared for a new quad. There's also plans for a new performing arts center and a new station for the regional passenger rail that runs to Nashville and Lexington. This block will be one of the most valuable stretches of real estate in the central city, nestled between two parks and two cultural centers, sitting by a commuter rail line. Rich liberals will eat it up."

Five of the eight homes in the connected row had been purchased back in the 1970s under a program that allowed people to buy the home for $1, and receive federally backed financing to renovate the homes. Owners who had had held onto the other three had long ago subdivided the buildings into apartments. A change of zoning in 1978 had converted the neighborhood back to single-family residential with a grandfather for existing structures – and that grandfather expired in six months. The best estimate was that the eight houses would cost us over a million dollars to buy, and the cost of renovating each would run over another million. If it worked out, we'd clean up. It would take all of our credit and all of our cash to make the job go.

"Are we the first ones in the neighborhood?"

"No, but we're the first ones on the block. Most of the single-project flippers are south of here or over on 5th Street, and some of those guys are working projects in the area that's about to get condemned. Look," he grasped my shoulder, "you've been on the road long enough, and you've been trapped up there in your head too long. It is time to build something. Here. Now. With me."

I paused, looked away, and looked back at Mike. "You're sure the line is across the street?"

"Yep. We need to finalize these deals within six weeks. Life's easier if we own the row. How long do you need to think about it?"

"You sure you want to do this?"

"Are you board-certified?"

I looked Mike in the eye. "Yes, I am board certified. And I don't need any more time. Let's do it."

So we went to work. Over the coming months we secured the properties and started to work on demolition and rehabilitation. There was plenty of work to keep me busy, and not a lot of time for distractions.

Mike reintroduced me to some of our friends from school and college, mainly informal stuff – lunch, drinks, and the occasional party at his house. It was good to get reacquainted, but fitting back in after you've missed a decade of people's lives is difficult.

I mainly stayed down by campus, working on the project. As we progressed on houses, I moved among them, sleeping in whichever unit had electric, water, and a clean room where the crews were not working. Every morning I'd take a run down the Olmsted-inspired parkways that linked the parks of the city. On Mondays, after checking on the project or meeting with Mike, I'd head over and do my one weekly lecture at U of L and then get back to the renovation.

Most weekends I worked, except to slip out and visit with my parents at their lake house on Taylorsville Lake. Dad had rebuilt the old dock on the lake, and we'd just cast off some lines and try to reel in some of the bass and crappie. We didn't talk much. We didn't need to. The company was enough.

III. The Beck and Call of Folks with Money

Chapter 13

Thanksgiving Day, Last Year

I WAS RUNNING LATE. Again. *As always*, my grandmother would say.

It was a humid day, and unseasonably warm for this late in the year. Thunderstorms were in the forecast for that afternoon. I had gone downtown to check on the electrical wiring in one of the units in advance of an inspection on Friday– the drywall guys were going to be closing up and mudding some walls in five of the houses and we couldn't afford to fail another inspection.

An accident on I-71 coming from the city tied up eastbound traffic for over an hour. Coming from the city to my Mam-Maw's place at Six Mile Creek, just up from the Landing, it was usually easier to head up I-71 and then drop down through Bethlehem. The rain stopped as I sat in the traffic, so I pulled back the top on my old Mustang and enjoyed the light breeze from the west as I headed out from downtown toward the country.

Thanksgiving dinner always started promptly at three. If I was too late I would be lucky to get a plate, let alone a place to sit. Every year, regardless of circumstance, the whole family was drawn back home for holidays, and Thanksgiving was the most important holiday of them all to Mam-Maw. There were no presents to exchange or religious rituals to be observed. Thanksgiving was about the kitchen, and food, and family being together. It was all of her family, her sons and daughters and in-laws and grandchildren pulled together beneath the secure roof of her little farmhouse near the river.

Mam-Maw was over ninety now. She used a walker and spent a lot of time sitting in her lift chair yelling at the television. She wouldn't move into an assisted living facility, and she never went anywhere to see anyone. Members of the family visited with her each day, and we paid my cousin Kay to stay with her at night as a sort of sitter. Helping to take care of Mam-Maw had become a daily routine for my uncles and aunts. She was content to have groceries delivered, cook her meals, and to lightly tend the house while the rest of the family passed through her kitchen. It was funny that she wouldn't go anywhere. She drove three million miles in forty years on rural mail routes, and I guess she figured she had traveled far enough. Life could come visit her for a change.

There would be thirty-eight for dinner this year. It was my first Thanksgiving back in thirteen years, since that last Christmas when I'd broken with Tara. I had no doubt that my aunts had started baking pies and pastries a week before. The yeast rolls had been rising all day before they went in the oven. There would be five types of salad and nine casseroles and pudding and iced tea so sweet and thick you could warm it up and pour it over your pancakes. The homemade preserves and apple butter put up during the summer would come out as a fall treat. My Uncle Orley would have smoked the turkeys, slow-roasting two big-breasted birds all night.

My Dad's three brothers and three sisters would be there, along with their spouses and children and grandchildren. My aunts, Jeanne and Marianne and Ellen and Gert and Sammy and Vonda, would all be busying in the kitchen, trying to pull together dinner under the critical and disapproving eye of Mam-Maw. Orley was also camped out in the kitchen, parking his stocky seventy-year-old frame on the kitchen stool by the hydrator, his wide striped tie already loosened from the collar of his checked, short-sleeved shirt. His wife, Ellen, said little but did a lot. It is not easy being a Catholic, Republican woman in a family of Baptist Democrats, especially being married to Orley, so she concentrated on good works and kept her thoughts to herself as he sat and spat and kept up his scatological running commentary. She was a big, robust woman, with a big personality, but she kept it tucked away when she came up the hill.

Dad's youngest brother, Caleb, was camped out in the garage beside the house. He was a shade-tree mechanic made good, and there was always work to be done. As often as not, even on holidays, all the men ended up in the garage, where you could talk and smoke and swear while Caleb worked on some project or another. That's also where we kept the whiskey. The others, my aunts' husbands and the various cousins with their spouses and children, would be scattered around the house, either playing cards on the sun porch, or watching football and visiting in the front parlor. The kids would play all over the place, scattered from the attic to the basement and all around the dell of the farm where the house sat. Uncle Warren, my Aunt Marianne's husband, would sit in the parlor, immersed in the paper until he went out to smoke a cigarette. Warren farmed down in Bullitt County, and other than tractors and crops, he didn't care to talk about much.

The road back to Mam-Maw's was ancient, a winding old cow-path that had gradually widened to accommodate carts, then wagons, and finally cars. The state paved it around 1945, which was about when my grandparents had bought the farm with Grandpa's GI Bill money. As I turned away from the new highway and started up the old road, I could feel the wheels grab at the pavement and my memory of driving the road came back. There were more houses now, many more than just a few years before, and they were large. A lot of the old tobacco growers had given up and quit planting, so a lot of the leased land was subdivided by heirs who had no use in their life for eighty acres of bottomland. As I made the last turn coming up the hill before Mam-Maw's driveway, I could already see the line of cars in the driveway and stretching out onto the street. I was the last one to show up.

The gravel of the driveway crackled under my tires as I pulled in and parked on the grass. The day had turned warm, so I shed my sweater and put the top up on the car. All the other cars were detailed, cleaned up to show off for the rest of the family. My Uncle Orley's Crown Victoria was parked at the top of the driveway, ready for a quick escape if he got an emergency call. Orley was the chief of the Cherokee County fire department, twenty trucks strong, and the car was a perk of the job. If an emergency call came through, he would be gone in a flash.

Over the years, I saw a lot of disasters from Orley's fire chief car. One Christmas, when I was about twelve, we were out in the garage when a call came through just after lunch. Orley and I and Daddy piled into the Crown Vic, and roared off down the old road doing about eighty. When we got to the main highway Orley opened it up to a hundred. There was a house fire down in the poor part of the county. By the time we got there two trucks, a pumper and a water-hauler, were already there along with about twelve volunteers. The house was half-burned. Fortunately everyone had gotten out, but the cavernous eyes of the three kids, and the look of hopeless desperation in the face of their mother, told the real story of loss and tragedy on a day of giving. Once the fire was out, Orley drove us back home, leaving the volunteer shift commander to handle the paperwork and look after any flame-ups. Other times we had seen a gas main explosion, a six-car pileup on I-64 that required the Jaws of Life, and a trailer fire. Of all the crazy disasters and emergency epics, the best had to be the afternoon of the Easter when I was fourteen and Orley climbed a radio broadcast tower, cigar between the teeth, to pull down a hung sky diver – and he's afraid to go up in airplanes and tall buildings.

Anyhow, I parked the car and walked around the side of the house toward the back door. Little cousins I'd never seen were playing around in the conifers beside the house, climbing up in them and playing tag games underneath like their parents and grandparents before them. Uncle Caleb was in the garage, smoking and talking with Mam-Maw's brother, Uncle Harley, and Grandpa's brother, Uncle Elvin. We lost Grandpa thirty years before.

"Hayden! Get in here!" Harley was motioning me into the garage. Caleb looked up from the hood of the Chevy he was working on, and wiped his hands on a rag. You wouldn't think it had been thirteen years since I'd been home, but last week, judging by the conversations and the familiarity.

"You're about late, Hayden," grinned Caleb. "Momma was wondering if you'd get here in time."

"Hey, traffic, you know." I didn't have a good explanation, "We didn't eat yet?"

"Just about to sit down. We've got time." Elvin this time. "So what've you been up to? Your Daddy says you've been traveling. That right?"

I reached over and grabbed Caleb's cigarettes from his shirt pocket and fished one out. Marlboro, gold packet.

"Yeah, a little. I was in Seoul, and did two years in Hungary after that."

"You back here to stay this time?" Uncle Harley asked as he lit me up.

"Don't know. Still have the place in New Orleans. I'll be here for a while. Helping a friend with a project downtown. What've you been up to?"

Harley demurred a moment. "Well, I was helping Clay out with his business for a little while, but now I'm mainly spending my days down at the cabin on Greene River, trying to get it back into shape. We didn't use it while Rosalee was sick, but now that she's gone I've got more time. Figure the place needs me around." Clay was Harley's oldest; his wife Rosalee had died the previous summer. I always liked them. Harley and Rosalee taught me to water ski when I was a kid.

A voice rang out from the back porch. "You little shits! Get in here and get washed up for dinner. And Caleb–" it was my Uncle Orley, "–tell that hippie artist that it's about time his sorry ass showed up here. His grandmama wants to see him!"

We headed across the yard drive to the house and up the back steps to the stoop and into the kitchen. Caleb walked beside me, a hand resting on my shoulder. "Sure glad you're back home boy. Now c'mon up and let everyone else have a crack at you."

Chapter 14

THANKSGIVING DINNER WAS EVERYTHING I had remembered from childhood. The food was delicious, and the conversation was nothing but gossip.

Daddy's family is an incorrigible group of gossipmongers, rumor-spreaders, and eavesdroppers. When he was young, Daddy said, his family had a party line with three other families on the road. The number of rings told you who the call was for, so no one had to answer your call. But, everyone knew when you had a call, and you couldn't call out when someone was on the line. When the neighbors had calls, my Mam-Maw and Aunt Gert would unscrew the talkie part of the receiver, and listen in on the neighbor's calls. My grandmother would scan the envelopes of the mail she delivered, and read through the thin envelopes. Once, when one of her son's girlfriends was getting letters from another boy in the Army, she intercepted all the letters and burned them instead of delivering them. Information was power, but, more important for the family, information was entertainment.

I sat in the dining room with my cousin Glynn and her girlfriend, finishing the remains of some pie and talking about what I had been doing in Hungary. They lived in the same part of the city where Mike and I were working, and they had done their share of house-flipping, so we had some fun discussing wainscoting and where to find quality wide-pine board for flooring. After the dishes were cleared, I went into the living room and sat down with Orley and Mam-Maw. My other men cousins were outside smoking cigarettes, and the women were either in the kitchen or managing the kids.

"So how are you, Hayden?" Orley asked.

"Fine, fine. Nice to be back home. It's been a while."

"Too damn long, you ask me. Did you see your kinky-haired Dad and Mom before they went out of town?"

"Yeah, visited when I came in from Atlanta." Mom had finally nagged Dad into taking a three-month trip to Belize. They were sitting on a beach somewhere, Mom sunning and Dad trying to get the NASCAR race results off of a Blackberry. "I'm staying out at the house in Vintners Landing on the weekends, but I need to be closer into the city during the week."

The rain had started outside, driving everyone into the house. Now there were forty wet, sweaty, stuffed people crowding Mam-Maw's little house. Harley came in and sat down with us. "Now what's this project again? I saw something about it in the paper last week. 'Style' section." A buddy of mine from high school was associate editor of the *Courier*, and had aimed a reporter our way as a favor.

"Well, what we're doing is we're taking a stretch down on Fourth, near the campus, and renovating eight old brownstones from condos and apartments, back into single-family residences. What we do is gut the inside except for the old floors. We remove every piece of the old finish carpentry work, every piece of original flooring or fixture, tag it, and store it. Then, working with the client, we develop a new interior that's in the architectural tradition of the original home. For seven of the houses we were able to find the old plans at the county courthouse."

"What's the cost on that? Sounds like a waste of time to live downtown." Orley grumbled to me.

I blew off the last part of the question, and smiled at him. "Ain't cheap, to be sure. We got a good deal on the property, but after renovation and restoration, each house will probably go for about $300 a square foot."

"So what's that work out to?"

I told him. The figure got everyone's attention. Rollins, they love money. "How many of you are partners in this thing?"

"Two of us."

"And you've got buyers for all the houses?" Harley asked.

"All but one, the one I've been staying in."

Aunt Ellen brought us some more coffee. Out in the kitchen, I could hear my Aunt Gert and her daughter, my cousin Laney, getting into an argument over some thing or another. We all rolled our eyes at each other, smiled, and drank our coffee. We'd heard the argument before.

"So, Hayden, you seeing anybody?" My Aunt Ellen knew better than to go back in the kitchen. She sat down and joined our little hidden conversation.

"No, not really." That much was true. I had not realized just how deeply in love I was with Tracy until she was torn away from me. The pain had faded, but I just hadn't found anyone in Seoul or Budapest who made me feel the way I had with her. There had been moments, or even nights, but nothing had overcome the memories of what I had lost.

"Hayden," Mam-Maw pulled my chin up and looked straight at, "we were all real sorry when you lost Tracy that way. She was a great girl, and we all know how much you loved her. I even understand why you went off the way you did. Your Grandpa was the same way at your age. Had to see the other side of the world to set his mind straight."

Harley chimed in. "But he couldn't keep running away, and you know you can't either. Now you're home and we're glad you're back with us. You've got to start living for what is next, not for what passed. You let us know how we can help."

I smiled around at them all. "Thanks." I'd probably had enough advice. I'd listen to Harley and my grandmother because they actually knew loss, and they were qualified to speak.

My Mam-Maw clasped my hand in her firm, arthritic grip. "We know."

Chapter 15

DINNER AND DESSERT WERE DONE. The kids were already picking at the leftovers when I went onto the front porch to have a smoke. The Green Bay game was on the television in the front parlor. Outside, the humid day turned cloudier. I went out and put up the top on the convertible. It had already gotten rained in once today.

When I came back in, the television interrupted football to report severe weather. There were tornadoes, mainly down in the city but also headed east. One of them looked big, maybe an F3, and was headed toward the general vicinity of Mam-Maw's farm.

Aunt Marianne came in from the kitchen, and laid her hand on Mam-Maw's shoulder. "We better get down to the cellar. Hayden, you help Caleb get Mama. Orley, can you get the boys from outside?"

Caleb and I picked up the legs and back of Mam-Maw's dining room chair and carried her down the narrow staircase to the cellar. It was quicker and easier to haul her than to let her walk down those stairs. Orley rousted the boys from the garage, and everyone else went down the back steps from the stoop to the outside door to the cellar. Ellen had brought Orley's fire department radio down from the kitchen. A bunch of the older folks gathered around the old TV in the basement corner. We picked up the broadcast from the NBC affiliate on the old rabbit ear antenna, which was of limited use, trying to watch a color radar display on a nine-inch black-and-white screen. Outside, the sirens sounded in the distance.

My cousin Glynn and I uncovered the old piano on the back wall of the cellar. It was badly out of tune and missing one pedal, but it was sufficient for playing old camp songs to keep the kids occupied. For an hour we belted out songs we had learned at YMCA camp and summer Bible school thirty years before, while the winds blew through the trees outside. In another corner Gert and Laney continued their argument about God knew what, evidently oblivious to the storm.

As the wind died off, Orley's fire radio went off and his cell phone started to ring. There were a lot of problems, a lot of accidents and damage in the area, and he needed to go to work. So, like on so many holidays before, Uncle Caleb and I ran out of the house and jumped in Orley's big fire chief car. Soon enough we were going ninety down the new road, Orley carefully avoiding blown limbs and scattered debris that littered the three-lane highway.

The first call was a collapsed house in Cropper. We were the second unit to arrive, after a fire-rescue truck. Orley sent Caleb around to shut off the gas line to the house. After the gas was shut off, we went stepping gingerly through the rubble of the wood-frame house, looking for any survivors. After about ten minutes we cleared away some of the half collapsed roof, and found the stairs going down to the basement. Orley and I used a pry bar to break away the stuck door from its frame, and then he ventured down with a flashlight and a walkie-talkie. Downstairs, the entire family was sitting around the basement, all safe and sound, and the new baby in the family was sound asleep.

Orley's radio went off again. There were three house fires, and trucks had been dispatched to all of them. But, the biggest problem was on the train line near Hatton. The train, headed west, was caught in the direct path of the biggest twister. So, we headed south and west, down Vigo Road.

The funnel had not disrupted the engine. However, the twister had taken an odd path, and had cut straight up a culvert, destabilizing a small trestle near Quisenberry Road. On the bridge itself, a rail had bowed. The westbound train approached the bridge at about forty miles per hour, and slowed as it crossed the trestle. The twister had taken out several of the cars, derailing them behind the fast-braking train. But, even a slow-moving train has a lot of throw weight. The lead engine followed the outward-bowed rail, dropping its other wheels and listed to the right. The engine then started to slowly turn perpendicular to the tracks, and then left the side of the trestle about three-quarters of the way across, falling almost a hundred feet. It pulled the other two engines after it.

The giant diesel-electric engine dove forward towards the last piling of the trestle, dislodging the main timber and partially collapsing the western end of the trestle. It continued forward, a hundred tons of train engine moving about twenty miles an hour, plowing into the loamy earth mixed with gravel and clinkers underneath the western end of the trestle.

The engineers were thrown clear from the wreck. One was killed immediately on impact with the ground, the other was hung up in the limbs of an old oak tree to the south of the trestle. Of the dozen or so derailed cars, seven came to rest below the trestle along with the other two engines. The car in the middle was a propane tanker. It broke on impact with the ground, but the gas leak did not ignite, leaving a potentially volatile situation for the emergency rescue teams on the scene.

We arrived at the train trestle not ten minutes after the call came in. The hazardous materials team from the Louisville fire department was on the way out. Caleb and I stayed back by the road, minding the electronic road flares set out to divert traffic. It would take days to clear away all the wreckage, and weeks to repair the trestle. This stretch of road would likely have to be closed until the propane carriers had been cleared. Once the propane tanker was secure, Orley called us over to check out the wreck. It was dark now, about nine o'clock, and another severe thunderstorm was rolling in. Lightning was starting to crackle overhead, and the rain had been coming down steady for the past hour.

We walked around the giant engine, which was resting on its side with its nose embedded in the western embankment of the gully. You can't appreciate how big a train engine is until you are right next to one, how heavy an engine is until you see the furrow one cuts in the ground when it derails at speed. Several small trees were snapped clean by the force of the train's motion. It looks like God's plow has been at work.

The water washed down the hillside from the top of the gull, bringing mud down from the scarred hillside. I stopped to smoke another cigarette with Caleb, hunching underneath the side of the engine. Then, I heard a voice calling out. "Chief, chief! Get up here."

Near the front of the train, one of the volunteer firefighters was standing on the nose, shining a flashlight around on the hillside. Orley went scurrying up the side of the train, and crawled forward on the nose to look closer. He turned and yelled back, "Hayden, get your ass up here and look at this!"

"What do you need me for?" I called back.

"Boy! Get up here! I need you now!"

I ran over the front of the train and climbed the slippery underside to get onto the nose of the capsized locomotive, where it had gouged the hillside near the pilings for the trestle. Orley grabbed my arm as I righted myself onto the top of the train.

"You were a cop once. I need to see if you think this is what I think it is. You're gonna need to crawl up under there a bit, under that great timber. Here," Orley shoved his flashlight into my hands, "look right there, to the left, over there. See that there? Under the wood, that plastic and paper?'

I crawled forward and leaned over the curve of the old engine's nose. There was a bunch of plastic and paper and tape, all wrapped up together. The paper and plastic was torn, evidently just torn. And staring back up at me was a human skull.

I flinched and jumped back, and started vomiting on my feet.

"That's what I thought too."

I turned my head and looked back at Orley. "Get some tarpaulins up here and cover this hole to cut down on any further damage to the area surrounding the body, and treat this like the crime scene that it is. Call the county police. We can't touch or move anything else until the detectives get out here."

We were at the crash until about eleven Thursday night. The NTSB guys had shown up, and were ascertaining the failure of the trestle and working out the order of events in the crash. We gave them a statement, told the cops on the scene about uncovering the remains, and then we left. I stayed the night at Caleb's, too tired to drive home and too unnerved to drink.

The next morning when I headed home, I made a stop, slowing at the turn on the way to Momma and Daddy's place, and pulled onto the blacktop in front of the Trattoria. Friday after Thanksgiving, and Sal was open for business at ten, as usual.

The old cowbell above the storm door clacked as I let the door shut. A voice, old yet not so, familiar and strange, sounded behind me "I'll be right out."

I turned to grab a Coke out of the cooler, then went to the counter and sat the drink by the cash register. My palms rested on the frosty windows to the icebox at the front of the register, filled with gelato flavors. Around me, the sausages and cheeses and baskets hung about, frozen in time. Looking to my right I saw Salvatore walk toward me from the kitchen.

"That all? Can I get you anything else?" he smiled as he untied the butcher's apron from his waist. Salvatore was still the same at fifty as he was at twenty, his hair was more gray and thinner, but his teeth still shone a smile ingrained by years in the restaurant business. He wore the same tan slacks and a grey flannel shirt he always did, and had a pair of black loafers on his feet. He hadn't changed at all since a time when I saw him every day.

"Hi Salvatore."

His eyes narrowed, the smile disappearing for an instance. "Hayden?"

I smiled, and nodded.

"Boy, it's been a dog's age." He grabbed my hand, pumping vigorously. "Son, I hear tell about you, but folks around here didn't think you'd ever come back! Are you visiting?"

"Actually, I'm here for a while. I'm staying out at Mom and Daddy's for a few weeks. Local job."

He smiled and looked down while he bagged my purchase. "Good, good. That place looks different, all empty and blacked out. It'll be good to see lights on again. By the way, how's your Momma? She doesn't come in much anymore, even when she's in town."

Mom spent most of the year in Hilton Head, while Dad came and went. For now, they were both in Belize.

I nodded my assent. "How's Miss Angina?"

"Mother? Oh, she's well enough, as well as can be expected. Some good days, some bad. She quit working a few years back, splits time between here and going to Gulf Shores with my older sister Lenore. She'll be back in April, once it gets too hot. Mama passed last year, you know."

I didn't know she had passed on. "I heard."

He handed me the Coke in the small paper bag. "So what brought you home? Business or family? Home for long?"

"Both. I have some work in the city. I'll be around. Look," I lied, "I'm expected, so I better get down the road. I'll drop in tomorrow."

I headed out the door and climbed back into my car. As I turned the engine over I throttled the accelerator and headed back east on Grapevine Road, toward Old Bard's Town Road and on to home. In my rear view mirror I saw Salvatore come out the front door and wave,

The farm loomed ahead, along with bed. I needed to get some rest; my cousin Doug and I were going hunting the next day, Saturday.

Chapter 16

KNOCK.

What the hell is that?

Knock-knock.

Why is someone knocking on the outside of the plane?

KNOCK!

"Wake up, Hayden, dang it all! We're late!"

I sat bolt upright on the couch, the muffled shout ringing in my ears. Out the back door I saw my cousin Doug, wearing an orange camouflage vest and holding his shotgun. Another orange vest was in his hand. "Hayden, we're late. You ready?"

I motioned him inside as I pulled on my boots. "Yeah, I'm ready . . . what time is it?"

"Four-thirty. We need to get moving to get out to the stand before dawn."

I pulled Dad's old shotgun off the mantle and stumbled out the door. I settled into the passenger seat of Doug's big pickup, and fell back asleep before he pulled out of the driveway. A few minutes later, I felt a bag land in my lap, and heard the sound of the road as we started moving, the sun just starting to come up behind us.

"Eat up. Brashear's was open so I stopped and grabbed some of those biscuits with sausage. Coffee's in the thermos." Doug had already devoured half of one of the sandwiches, and was pouring a cup of coffee while he drove. "Thought we'd go down to Peytona, head out above the big houses and hunt from Papaw's stand on the old Dixon place."

"Sounds good." I mumbled as I closed my eyes for a last couple of minutes' rest.

About twenty minutes later we wheeled up to the old highway bridge. The teenagers were gone, their beer cans and burned out roaches in the concrete, and the fishermen hadn't shown up yet. Another truck pulled in behind us, with Bubba McDonald and Terry Wayne. Mike was already there too. After a couple of minutes of the obligatory country boy bullshit and a check of our gear, we headed out along the ridge to the west of the Fork, behind the big new development, Butcher's Block, going south, into the wind.

About a half-hour later we got to the old deer stand, back on Papaw's timber farm off Dix's Port Road. The land had been in the family for years, but there was no easy way to get to the old stand. Papaw had sold off parts, and left the farm in three sections. Papaw had sold the part across the interstate, to the south. None of the neighbors wanted the smaller part to the east, and there was no road to it. An easement gave us access, but there was no use in developing it, so we kept it wild, our own 50 acre preserve for game. We camped there when we were kids, walking along the tracks, and partied there as teenagers. Now we hunted there, adults headed for middle age with lost ambitions and plenty of old lies to tell.

It wasn't so much a stand as it was a camp. The foundation to the old farmhouse was there, along with the fireplaces and chimneys from Papaw's old house. When the house burned back in '47, he hadn't taken them down. He wanted to rebuild closer to the Beaver Bridge Road, so he moved the family to the other end of the farm, leaving behind the old house and the old memories.

Doug still kept a cord of firewood at the "old house" and he had added the frame for a large tent across the highest part of the foundation. He had come out on Friday to drop the gear we needed, saying he didn't want the trucks to scare off the game. The deer stand was at the other end of the farm, 700 yards away. After we stowed our gear at the camp, Doug and I headed for the stand, and, by the time we climbed into the stand, the sun was cracking the horizon.

The morning passed without event. No game in sight. Terry bagged a couple of rabbits after lunch, and that night we roasted them over the fire and played pinochle over whiskey and beer. By about eight we were telling lies about girls we used to know.

"Shit," it was Terry, "remember that sassy stacked girl what used to live down the road from you! God, what was her name? Had them big ole thangs there?"

"Where?" Doug mumbled as he poured more whiskey into his Coke. Despite his affectations, Doug was actually a pretty successful attorney in Carritherston. He had gotten his degree in the army and found a niche in real estate law and family law after he left the commonwealth's attorney's office two years ago.

"Down at the old green-roofed house. Jamie? No–"

I slid my cap back over my eyes. "You mean Jenny?"

"Shit, that's right! Jenny Barnes. Sassy gal. Man, I done went after that one night – Ow! "

"Lying sack of shit!" Doug laughed. He had tossed an empty Coors can across the fire, right into Terry's forehead. "She was too damn busy chasing around with your daddy to have any time for you. You might have dreamed it, but she wouldn't have done you for money."

Mike fell over laughing, and reached for a bottle. "Don't matter anyway. She got knocked up senior year, moved down to Somerset or some other place with her boyfriend. Hear that they're still together."

"Grandma Jenny ..."

I started to doze off.

"Hey, Doug, remember ..."

After a day and a night in the woods, in a cold rain, and with little luck, we hung it up and headed back to civilization. Orley had left a message on my cell phone, to drop by. Terry's truck was hung up in the mud and we couldn't get it out, so we all piled into Doug's truck and headed over to Orley's. We figured to hit Aunt Ellen up for breakfast, and then we would go fetch Caleb's Jeep and pull Terry out of the mud.

About six o'clock Sunday morning we pulled into the gravel path leading to Orley and Ellen's place near Carritherston. The house started as a little two-bedroom bungalow, and then they closed in the patio and added a new kitchen. Orley had then added a bedroom and a family room. The end product was the most unlikely looking house in the county, encompassing three architectures: Picasso meets rural eclectic, expressed as home.

We looked for all of our worth like a group of refugees. Ellen came out of the sliding glass door from the kitchen. She has an infectious smile and a big, robust body to go with her big, robust personality that she exhibits when not at Mam-maw's. She came out onto the yard and grabbed Doug and me around the shoulders and hugged us both. "Boys! Haven't seen you in forever! Haynie, we hoped you'd come up for a spell, honey. Get inside."

"Couldn't imagine otherwise," I smiled. "I'll be around a lot."

"Now get out of those boots and jackets, and get cleaned up. I'll have breakfast rustled up in about ten minutes. Coffee's on the stove."

The inside of the house was warm and inviting. After we cleaned up and settled in at the table, Ellen paused from her ongoing monologue about family, friends, and food. "Now what happened that has you boys out getting all cold and wet?"

"Deer." Her look was enough of an answer. Ellen asks no foolish questions, and answered stupid questions with a look that said as much. The other guys chimed in, adding bits and pieces about what happened and how their families were. The conversation waxed and waned with the servings of food. In the background, a police scanner interrupted with periodic dispatches from around the county.

Through the open patio windows, the sound of the slacking rain gave way to gravel crackling under car tires. I looked and saw Orley's Crown Vic pulling up the drive. "There he is, the old liar," Ellen grinned, "give him a few minutes to get ready. Won't have that, have that old fool mess up these floors." Years ago she had made Orley start hosing off before he could come in from a fire. After forty years it was ingrained habit, regardless of the weather. We all looked at our feet guiltily. "Now boys, you're family but you're company. If I let Orley get by one day I'll never get this house straightened up! It took me forever to break him in." She prepared another plate and set it at the head of the table.

The back door to the kitchen slid open and Orley limped in, a fresh cigar between his teeth. The civil engineers were out inspecting the damage from the fire. The trestle would be unusable for at least a couple of weeks. We exchanged more idle chatter about hunting and family. My cousin Sheila was back home with Orley and Ellen, another failed marriage in her pocket and two children in tow. They would all be up soon, so I would of course have to stay around after breakfast to visit and make nice with the strangers in my family. Doug and the boys made their thanks and headed out the door to fetch Doug's truck. I poured another cup of coffee and listened to one of Orley's racial conspiracy theories. Then, about seven-thirty the phone rang.

"Orley! Jethro's on the phone."

"No need to shout! I'm here. Jethro? Yes. What – yeah we'll be right there." Orley handed the phone back to Ellen. "C'mon Hayden. Looks like this thing just got interesting."

"What?"

"I'll tell you in the car. I can drop you over at the house when we get done."

As we tore out of the driveway, Orley tossed his cigar out the window. "The structural guys from the railroad and the civil engineer said that part of the embankment that gave way two days ago, that they had rebuilt it back in 1991. That body? Forensics' initial reaction is that it's a teenage girl."

My eyes jerked off the road and stared at Orley.

Steering with one hand, his other went into the console for another Roi-Tan. Bite the nub, spit it out the window, and start talking again. "Yeah, they think it's a girl, but it's been there for a while. Really decomposed. They need a formal statement –"

I muttered a reply without thinking, "About how the body got uncovered. Makes sense. They could have come to the house for that." I was bone cold and tired, and just wanted to go to bed.

"Hayden, if I gotta go out and do this, you do also; just because you got out of this business, don't tell me it ain't goddamn interesting."

I looked back at the road, jaw set. "Oh fuck you old man."

Orley threw his head back laughing, and slapped me on the knee with his free hand. "Goddamn you're easy to set off! Pappy was right that you got no sense of humor. Why are you always so dark, so closed off from everyone? I just thought you might see something useful." An uncomfortable pause followed. "Look, you were a good cop. These jokers can always use another set of eyes. Don't forget, your Papaw was one of the best cops this town ever had. You got some of him in you."

"Beginner's luck. I build houses now."

We parked at the west end of Quisenberry Lane and caught a ride out with a police search and rescue vehicle, jostling over the ties in the railroad bed. About five minutes later we were back where the bridge crossed a creek that fed into the Fork.

What had been, two days earlier, a quiet patch of rural timberland dissected by the tracks was transformed. NTSB and police SUVs were perched on either side of the creek, and a TV helicopter circled overhead.

Across the trestle, a collection of police and rescue personnel gathered around the side of the collapsed embankment. Yellow crime scene tape was stringed around some stakes and trees near the tracks. Inside the tape, a team from the coroner's office was extracting the corpse and preparing to transport it to the morgue. A short, dark man in a hunting jacket walked towards us as we finished crossing the bridge. TV crews lingered, looking at a slow news weekend until now.

"Morning, Chief."

"Morning. Hayden, this is Detective Augustus Ellis. Gus, meet my nephew, Hayden."

He nodded. "Hayden. Gentlemen, if you'll come this way, I'll fill you in on what we have."

We walked down the embankment and stepped over the crime scene tape, mud and grass slopping up on us.

"Here's an apparent homicide victim, female, probably in her late teens. Coroner's report should tell us more. We can't be sure how long she was buried, but it has probably been some time. The civil engineer is on the phone trying to get information about maintenance and construction on this trestle, but it'll be a while. NTSB isn't saying anything yet."

He continued. "The body was wrapped in what looks to have been paper, like butcher paper, and then wrapped again in plastic. She hadn't completely decomposed, so–"

"There might still be good physical evidence," I interjected.

Ellis looked back, expressionless. "Exactly. Good call. Who are you again?"

"Hayden Rollin."

"You a cop?"

"Was, once. Two years, NOPD homicide."

Gus looked me up and down. "Okay. We can probably come up with a good identification, if we can come up with an approximate year of death. Figure she's probably a runaway, so a computer search through missing persons can come up with likely candidates. Then, we start matching dental records. Then the really hard work starts. I doubt that we can figure out who did this thing, even if we get good forensic evidence."

"Time?"

"Time. Most anybody could have done this, and if she was a drifter we might never find out. But–"

Uncle Orley broke the silence. "But what, Gus?"

"Well, Orley, if the girl is from around here we might figure something out. Just takes time."

We talked a few more minutes, and Gus walked us back to one of the county police SUVs. I reached in my pocket for my wallet and pulled out a card. "Gus?"

He stopped and turned back around. "Yes?"

I scribbled my cell number on the back of the card. "I'm staying out at my momma's place for a little while, over on Old Bard's Town Road. Call me when you find something out."

"Sure. Look, I was going to have a deputy go out to take another statement. Why don't I drop by tonight, and I'll fill you in?"

"No problem. We're on Old Bard's Town Road, off Grapevine after you pass through Vintners Landing. If I'm not at the house, go next door to my aunt's place, Mrs. Hunter. I might be over there."

Gus nodded and I closed the door to the Blazer. It was starting to rain again as we left.

Chapter 17

AFTER ORLEY DROPPED ME OFF at home I slept. I didn't have any obligations in the city until late on Sunday, so I got up about noon, and then pulled the old Mustang down to the garage to give it an overdue overhaul from the trip up from Atlanta.

Old cars are funny. They can run almost without fault, even over long distances, especially if they are called upon to do the same none-too-strenuous tasks over and over again. But, then the smallest thing can happen that stresses the system and the whole thing just breaks down and you never get it back together again. The thing I kept reminding myself was that this car was as old as me. I couldn't run the way I did in high school, so the car was actually one leg up on the driver.

The rains had stopped, and the day was cool. After I opened the garage door and pulled the car in, I looked around and found Dad's old coveralls hanging on the back of the door. I slid the coveralls on over my shorts and shirt, popped an old Willie Nelson eight-track into the stereo on the shelf, and started to tinker while the Red Headed Stranger played over the cheap Radio Shack speakers hanging in the rafters. First check all the fluids, top the coolant and brake fluid, and change the oil and filter. Air pressure, okay. The timing seemed a little off coming up from Atlanta. Pull out the timing light, check it and adjust the timing chain. Pull the plugs, check the ends, replace them. Ah, there's a small crack in the distributor cap; replacement's on the shelf. Might as well replace the cables. Generator and solenoid are good.

I knocked off from the job at about 2:30, pulled a beer out of the fridge by the tool bench and sat down on the driveway looking down at the pond. The clouds were blowing out, and the day was going to be clear. My appointment at the university was at four, so I went up to the house and got showered and changed. A sunny day meant I could leave the top down on the drive downtown.

The Sunday meeting downtown was uneventful, just a meet-and-greet with the administration and foundation at the university. The basketball coach was there, working a few of the potential foundation donors who had come by to look at the plans for the campus expansion. An NCAA championship does wonders for fundraising, and the team looked solid to make another run at the Final Four.

The redevelopment would affect property by campus, and the administration had an interest in the direction of redevelopment downtown, because it would influence their long-term master plan for the campus. I had been invited to run a short seminar on recent developments in what's called "organic" or "piece planning," and part of the deal was that I would also explain to the administration the nature of our redevelopment project and how it would benefit the campus. That Sunday I was doing a "donors and friends" roundtable for the people who gave the money that put names on brick and mortar. It wasn't that large an affair, but the honorarium for three meetings would pay the mortgage for a couple of months.

I didn't get away from the campus until almost six. Eastbound traffic on the interstate tied me up for the better part of an hour on the way home. By the time I got out to the farm, it was after seven, and Judith and Pepper, Doug's folks, would have already sat down for supper. I drove past momma's place and went straight to Judith's driveway. No sooner had I walked in the door that all of the kids of my cousins, Doug and Steve, had tackled my legs and were pulling at my arms. "Uncle Haynie, Uncle Haynie!" I hoisted the youngest up and dragged the two boys along on my legs as I passed through the parlor of the old house to the kitchen.

"Haynie! Baby! Get in here." Judith is a tiny woman, all wiry muscle and teeth, usually clinched around a cigarette. "Sounds like you boys had an adventure, judging by the news."

"News?"

"Yeah, buddy, your train wreck is on all the stations." Uncle Pepper had retired on disability years ago, but still worked as a welder out of his garage. "All the channels have shots of the farm and the embankment. Why didn't you tell us about that body?"

"Sorry Pep, I just sacked out when I got home, and then I didn't see you before I went to town."

"Body? What's the body Peepaw?"

"Never you mind boy. We'll tell you after dinner. Go get your daddy and tell him to get washed up."

Dinner went fast: venison steak and fresh vegetables, and a big pitcher of iced tea. Doug and Pepper went out on the front porch to smoke, while Judith and Doug's wife Kenna finished the supper dishes. The kids went off to watch television. I went out front and sat on the stoop, taking in the early evening breeze.

"Haynie, what'd you see out there." Pepper muttered as he lit another Lucky.

I sat for a moment, and collected my thoughts. "It's sad, Pep, real sad. Young girl, maybe sixteen or so, that's a guess, wrapped up and buried in the embankment. She had to have been there a while, judging by the deterioration of the corpse."

"Wonder where she was from?"

"Shoot, Daddy, does it matter? She's dead." It was Doug's brother Steve.

"Now, I know I raised you better than that, Steve. Imagine that Kay disappeared one day, and for ten years you didn't know what happened. You turn on the TV and they find an old corpse, and you just have to wonder … is it her? Know I would. Know I would."

Steve kept his mouth shut. He had always been like that when he knew he was wrong. He would just clam up and not say a word, and instead just stare at whatever was in front of him. "Look, Pep, we don't know anymore than the TV. I need some more tea." I stalked back into the house, and looked out the back window toward the pond, momma's place nestled just across the water in the far turn in the road. Cars were coming and going, either headed out for the night or coming home from evening services.

About an hour later, I was playing a video game with the older boy, Rance, when I heard a car out front. Pepper leaned his head in the door. "Hayden! Some nigger out here to see you."

I paused for a minute, and walked to the front door. A Ford Taurus sat in the drive, with state plates. Gus Ellis leaned on the front fender, talking into his radio. I grabbed Pepper, and whispered in his ear. "Old man, that man is a police detective."

"Still a nigger. Do your business out front." And Pepper headed in the house, doubtlessly knowing that the wrestling matches were coming on.

"Hello Detective."

"Hello, Mr. Rollin. I haven't interrupted your supper, have I?"

Doug leaned in. "You need me?"

"Nope. Go on in."

I turned back to Gus. "Call me Hayden, detective. No interruption at all. I was about to head home, just next door." I motioned to our house at the other end of the dell, a half-mile down the road. "Come on and we'll talk."

"Good idea."

I walked Gus out onto the screened porch that looks out over the pond. He settled into an old rocker while I hustled some cold beers from the bar fridge in the basement.

"They're cold, though I can't speak to the quality. They've probably been in there since about 1993."

Gus grinned back at me. "That's fine. Tell me about the wreck."

"It's all in the report that Orley is working up. That's it."

"You hunt back there?"

"Me? Not much, maybe ten times in my life. Doug and I were out there yesterday, but we were over by our stand, a half-mile west. When we were kids we went back there to party and camp, but I haven't been in those woods in almost fifteen years. Why do you ask?"

Gus looked down at his notes. "Just curious."

"Liar."

"Excuse me?" The detective nearly bolted out of his chair.

"You heard me. Liar. I've interrogated people too, detective, and I know you're lying, and I know you're interrogating me."

Gus gave me the look that said *so you want to play.*

"All right. I need to know things. You're from around here. You know things. You can help me learn things about this part of the county that I don't know, which might help me out. I've been on this for about three months – transferred from the Lexington police department. My wife's a doctor at Jewish Hospital in Louisville. I played ball at Cherokee County, but I'm from Silerville – wrong side of the county. There's history that matters to this investigation, maybe. You know it, I don't. I need to learn about this side of the county."

"There's a lot you can know without needing history."

"Like what?" Gus eased back in the rocker, set to listen.

"There's no doubt that body was put there on purpose. We know that girl was put there on purpose. Had to be done when the trestle was being built, or repaired. That means either a hundred years ago or fifteen years ago. Too much work to get those big timbers out and place that body back in there. Now–" I settled back in my chair as the detective started to relax, "that trestle is a century old. Thing is, those embankments had to be rebuilt and reinforced. I wager that you have an idea when that happened, and that's why you're nosing around here – because that body hasn't been there all that long."

"You sure?"

"That's obvious. They didn't make plastic wrap in the 19th century, and they also didn't make swatches. She's from the 1990s."

Gus eyed me. "What Swatch?"

"The one that was on her wrist. All the girls were wearing them in high school. I saw it when Orley and I secured the scene. Check your inventory. It ought to be there."

Gus Ellis took a long draw off his beer and sat the can on the table beside me. Leaning forward, he rested his elbows on his knees, and looked me dead in the eye. "It's there. You are an active watcher. That's good. Now be an active listener. You're right, I do have an idea. It's just a hunch now, and pretty soon I expect to have it confirmed. But I'm gonna need your help."

"Meaning?"

"I checked you out this morning. An honest cop in New Orleans, which is rare. And, you were a good cop before you got shot and got scared. Then you lost your wife." He paused, and considered his hands a moment, and then looked up. "What I didn't know, until today, is how close you are to this department, and potentially to this case. All the cops in the county knew your grandpa, half were related to you. The rest knew someone in your family. That body was basically in your backyard. And, unless I miss my guess, that young woman ended up in that hill when you were growing up here."

I sat upright, and looked straight back at the detective. "Gus, are you saying I did this? That I did this?"

"No. That is not what I said. But, I think you can help me out here, help me talk to people who are around here. I'm new here, but I am a veteran homicide investigator. I don't like this case, and I see lots of impediments to getting at the truth. But maybe, just maybe, we can figure out who lost a daughter, and figure out who took her."

"Fine. I just want to make sure that you don't find me to be a person of interest. But what do you want to know?"

"Tell me about growing up out here."

"Am I a person of interest?"

"No. Tell me about this side of the county fifteen years ago."

"That could take a while? Another drink?"

"Coffee." It was time to work. Gus got a primer on Vintners Landing.

Chapter 18

AFTER THE DISCOVERY OF THE REMAINS on Thursday evening, the search for an identity had commenced. A lot had happened between the time Orley and I found that corpse and when Gus showed up at my parents' place Sunday night.

The inquiry by the county police into missing persons and runaways from the tri-state area had uncovered no fewer than 9,000 reports for the year leading up to December 2007. Of those reports, about half were juvenile missing persons, and of that nine in ten were resolved or closed. There were 373 unresolved juvenile missing person cases in the tri-state for that period. That was a healthy number of cases to work through and narrow down.

Examination of the skeletal remains indicated that she had a shattered jaw, a fractured pelvis, and based on the breakage of her sternum, she had been stabbed at least once with a large knife. Metal filings from the knife were still evident on the sternum. It had been a vicious beating, a brutal assault where she was likely beaten before she was stabbed.

Fortunately, despite the damage to the skull and jaw of the remains, there was a largely intact lower jaw and a completely intact upper plate, minus two teeth that were knocked loose. Dental impressions from the remains were fed into the national forensic database. A 90% match was returned on a local runaway, filed in September 1991.

The balance of physical data presented a challenge. Over the coming days the medical examiner's office worked through the days and nights on the case. There was dried blood on the remains of the clothing and also on the plastic and paper remnants the body was found in. Some of the blood was the victim's, and some came from at least one other person. Partial prints were still evident on the interior of the plastic, preserved in a dried smear of blood. The prints had not produced a match in the national database.

The medical examiners had very nearly missed the most critical piece of information. As they catalogued the physical evidence of the remains, they collected and catalogued several shards of bone from the broken sternum and broken pelvis. In scanning items for a computer rendering to reassemble the pelvis and sternum to further assess the nature of the assault, two bone fragments were unable to be placed by the computer rendering. Closer examination revealed that the bones were a tiny femur and a tiny collarbone, two of the first bones to develop in the first trimester of a human fetus. DNA testing from the remains matched both the corpse and the dried blood on the interior of the plastic sheeting.

She had been pregnant, maybe two months along. And, based on the DNA testing, it appeared that the blood of the father was on the inside of her makeshift burial shroud.

The Sunday paper carried a story about the discovery of the body subsequent to the Thanksgiving Day tornado and crash. Orley and I were mentioned in the story, but no further mention was made of the identity of the corpse.

Monday morning I headed back into the city. I had to clear my gear out of the last of the old brownstones so we could complete renovation, and there were more meetings with inspectors related to the final rewiring. I would be spending most of my nights out at the house in the country, commuting in every day to coordinate with the subcontractors or meet with Mike and the bankers and real estate agents.

There were decisions to make, at least one of which was whether or not I was going to come back into property development for good. It had been good to work with my hands again, to deal with a tangible project and see ideas turned into brick and mortar and wood and granite. Mike was talking about a new project – turning the old Iron Works on the Ohio River into high-end lofts. We would likely have enough capital and reputation coming out of this project that we could secure the financing. There was a revitalization of downtown underway that made loft space potentially attractive. Come February, at the latest, I would have to commit to coming home.

I had finished packing up the last box – music, books, clothes – and sent Mike's assistant Walter to take them out to the house in Vintners Landing when the office phone rang.

"Hayden! Call for you downstairs! A Tara Gilliam."

"Who?"

"She said you'd know her as Tara Spencer."

My heart rose and sank at the same time. From time to time, in the back of my mind, I had wondered how Tara's life had turned out. I had no doubt that she had probably done well in life, if only because she possessed a drive for success and an appreciation of finer things that, when combined with her beauty and sexuality, made her attractive to people who could give her things. But there was that dark, brooding, controlled side. I had not heard from her since that last night together, and I surely had no idea she was still in town. Now, at the beginning of December, she had called me. It was a very brief conversation.

"Hayden?"

"Yes."

"It's Tara. Hayden, please come see me."

I said *yes*, took down the address and hung up the phone.

Mike was standing in the door when I hung up. "So you're going to talk to her this time?"

"Never you mind Mike. Just never you mind."

On the way home, I stopped at Salvatore's and picked up some roasted lamb and dried apricots, and a cold Coke. We chatted a bit, and in passing I asked about Tara. He said he hadn't seen her in almost ten years, but he was pretty sure she was still in town.

Chapter 19

THE FOLLOWING MORNING, I LEFT the job site at about ten and drove out highway 42 toward Shiloh and the great house with Tara in it. There was a small gift for her in the back of the car and many questions in my head.

The night before, I'd had Mike and his wife Lynn out to Vintners Landing. Lynn briefed me on Tara. As we had sipped wine after dinner, she laid it all out. Tara *had* done well.

"Hayden, I didn't even know you knew Tara. She's quite a story. A lot of us knew her as a personal buyer with Byck's, and later as the travelling buyer for Hytken's down in Saint Matthews. As I understand it from the ladies at the club, there was a party at Jim Porter's Tavern just before the Kentucky Oaks about five years ago. That's where she met Daemon Gilliam. I don't know if you knew the Gilliam's, but they're old money and had some success in horses."

"I know of them. His father owned part of the breeding syndicate on Secretariat."

"Yes, that's them. More wine? Anyhow, Daemon was older, and his family had come out of the New York horse crowd to Kentucky. Most of their money was in oil stocks and other derivatives; horses and the high life were the family passion. If you know Tara, you know she always liked a party, and she and Daemon, they had hit it off immediately. Daemon was just out of his third marriage, and I think they filled needs for each other. They were married by the next spring. And she's been holding court at the club every Thursday since."

No doubt, I thought to myself. Daemon likely afforded the sense of security and maturity that Tara found attractive, and she was smart and fun and sexual, which appealed to the needs of a divorced man of fifty.

Lynn filled in the rest of the blanks. Tara had left Hytken's, and set her own course in retail fashion, opening a boutique in Holiday Manor. Within five years her sense of style and business acumen made the store a success. No trophy wife life for Tara – she was going to succeed. She opened stores in Lexington, Louisville, Cincinnati, Memphis and Nashville, making Tara's East Side a regional name for the fashionable upper class. As Lynn described it, Tara's life was a ribbon of trips in her Audi, driving along the white-fenced roads through horse country to check her stores, flights to New York or Paris to buy for the stores, and checking with the caterer or the groundskeeper as to the needs for the next party. Moving into the "horsey set" came with a cost, though. She rarely saw her family, if she cared to do so. Life was her business, Daemon's parties, the club, and the Keeneland sales. The currency of power was gossip and controversy and predatory sexual politics.

The house was out on the riverfront, up past the country club near Shiloh. After I turned off old 42, I headed through the small postcard town and looked for the turnoff to Gilliam Pointe Farm. Set back on a long driveway, the house was a nineteenth century mansion done in the antebellum style. Poplars lined the brick drive that wound up to the front. White columns framed the red brick exterior, and horses ran in the wet morning fields. A grey sky hung overhead, creating a brooding quality that matched the mood of the river in the background.

I don't like to dress up, but this day I did. The horsey set plays by different rules and standards, and one of the rules is "dress like you have something else to do." So, as this was a social call, I dressed for what was ostensibly my next appointment – meeting with the bank. So I was in grey flannel and tie, with a blue overcoat and my best custom boots.

The housekeeper met me at the door and escorted me through the house to the sunroom in back. *So,* I thought, *this is not a formal meeting.* Were it business, we would meet in the study I passed at the front. A formal social visit, we would meet in the living room or the sitting room. This was something more personal, a family matter or other matter.

Heather – the housekeeper's name was Heather – took my overcoat and scarf and left me to the room. I sat the package I had brought along to the side, and stood to look out on the barges as they crawled up the river for Pittsburgh, laden with ore for the steel mills.

"Hayden."

Tara had entered the room so quietly I had not even heard her. She was just behind me, just out of reach. I turned to see that time had left her strikingly beautiful. Her hair had deepened to a chestnut color. It still hung to her shoulders. She was still slim and athletic. She radiated the easy confidence of a person of society.

"Tara. How are you?"

She took my hands and looked at me. "Well, quite well. But I should ask you as much. From what I hear. And I'm sorry to hear about your wife. Terry?"

"Tracy. And thank you."

"Coffee? Tea?"

"Tea. Please."

We walked over to the sofa beside the fireplace. She served and we chatted, me about losing Tracy and my travel, she about the business and Daemon. I gave her the gift – a watercolor of Tracy's, one of the better works she did. Rain fell outside as the grey sky turned darker, and the horses galloped across the field below, headed for the cover of the trees.

"Tara?"

"Yes Hayden?"

"Why am I here?"

"You tell me. Why are you here?"

The question took me aback for a moment. I get taken aback a lot, it seems. I collected my words, looked her straight in the eye, and spoke.

"I'm here because I'm sorry. Because on some level I cared for you and all I did was make you unhappy in my selfishness. I'm here because you asked me to come. You never before asked me to come."

Her smile evaporated the last of my apprehensions. "Set aside all that. You were good to me when no one else was, and you were fun, and we were young. It also isn't why I called you."

"Why, then?"

It was her turn to pause. She stared out the window, past me and even beyond the horses and the river. "I'm worried. And I think you are the only person who can help."

"Worried? About what?"

"I saw the article in the paper last Sunday about the body they found near the train track. I saw your name in the story."

It was my turn to control the conversation. I leaned forward, closing the distance as she still looked out toward the horizon. "I don't know why that would worry you. Orley and I were at my grandmother's when the accident call came in, and I went with him. I was with the firefighters who found the remains, that's all of my involvement. I'm not in any trouble. There was no danger."

"I didn't mean you. Look, you were gone for so many years. There is so much you did not experience, so much you missed being gone from here." She finally turned to me. "There is so much you did not hear. Stories swirl around this city like smoke in the winds, but they never blow away."

"Go on."

"Hayden. Oh, Hayden. There's only one person around who knew my family like I did: you. I've spent these years distancing myself from them and their sad anger, but the stories still made their way to me. All those years, people talked about how Salvatore behaved towards the teenage girls who come in the restaurant– he flirts with them, teases them. I never believed that he was, well, you *know*, but there was that one teenage girl, back before I came here. Mama used to talk about it when she was off her head on her medications, before she died. But Miss Angina and Mama denied it, my sister Lenore, she denied it. Hayden, I need to know – is that girl in the embankment Lana Rae?"

"Why? Why should you care?"

"If it is Lana Rae, then there will be a scandal. I just know it. I cannot afford a scandal. My entire life until I was twenty-five was dominated by the dysfunction and anger of my family. My mother attracted violent men, my grandmother attracted violent men. I –"

"Do you attract violent men?"

"Yes. But I put them at a distance. I learned to identify them early, and to be rid of them before they got close."

"Did I get too close? Was I too violent?"

"No. The problem was that you represented a different kind of threat – blind affection. Naïve, blind affection. But you also couldn't control yourself – we were good together, in bed. But with you, affection was control, and it was as dangerous to me as the threat of violence. I had never experienced that, and it scared me. I didn't love you, but I needed something like what you offered. Had I stayed with you, resentment would have set in. You would have figured it out. My experience said men don't want to be played fools, and all the men I had known turned violent when women played them. Why should you have been any different?"

I had nothing to say. I was embarrassed. She continued.

"Hayden, if you ever cared for me, you'll help me – I need to keep away from this scandal. But, it's about family, so I can't just do *nothing*. I cannot afford to let Salvatore go down. If that was Lana Rae in that earthen bank, then he might well have killed her. Or, he might not have. He's old now. He spent his entire life being beaten down by Mama and my mother. If he did it, I need to help him, get him a lawyer, help him run, whatever. But I need an intermediary." She reached for my hand, took it in hers. "I *need* you."

A half-hour later, I was headed back into the city, humidity fogging my convertible's rear window and words bouncing through my head. *Is that girl in the embankment Lana Rae? If that was Lana Rae in that earthen bank, then he probably killed her.* And *I need you.*

I need you.

I need you.

No one had needed me for three years. I finished up some work at the brownstone – end of the month meant checking accounts payable – and looked over the work of the tile contractor. There was also a post-it from Mike saying we had passed electrical inspections. About seven I headed east toward the Landing and home.

Chapter 20

GUS SHOWED UP AT THE HOUSE again on Wednesday night at about nine. We ate some barbeque he'd brought from a joint on Carritherston Road, and talked about the forensics of the case some more. Gus and I had walked down to the dock on the pond. An unseasonably late Indian summer was still trying to assert itself, and it was warm enough that we could wear shirtsleeves.

"Tell me about 1991."

"Well, the Braves won the NL pennant."

"Hayden, look, you know what I mean. Tell me about 1991. What was going on around here? Who'd you spend time with?"

"I wasn't hanging around this part of town so much. I was mainly hanging out near LaGrange and Prospect. I had drifted away from most of the kids out in this part of town, started hanging around the suburban kids from church."

"You were a religious kid?"

I stifled my laughter. "Hardly. Those kids in the suburbs, they fit my style, my interests. I was pretentious and wanted to be rich. They were going to college, and they wanted something besides a doublewide and a pickup. I didn't want to be a redneck."

"Tell me about the kids out here. Anybody disappear, start acting strange?"

"Gus, that's a long time ago. Let's see. '91. Well, that's the year that Danny got killed by Tyler Bridges."

"Danny?"

"Danny Cahill. His family owns the restaurant, the Trattoria, which you passed on the way out here. He got in an argument with his brother and tried to stab him. Sheriff's deputy shot him after he barricaded himself in the store and started shooting. Ask my cousin Scotty. He was there."

"Scotty?"

"Sergeant Scotty Guth at the state police. He's my cousin."

"Scotty's your cousin too? Another cousin on the force. Hmm. Okay. When was that?"

"About this time of year. November. Lets go back to the house."

We made our way back up to the house. Gus walked over to the front of the kitchen, looking out the window. He rubbed his shaved scalp with his free hand, a cup of coffee in the other.

"Hayden," Gus said out the window, "did you know a girl named Lana Rae Barnes?"

"Lana? Oh yeah,. Yeah, sort of. You drove by the house she lived in, about a mile back up the road. Blonde, quiet. I'm not sure if anyone really knew Lana Rae. She really kept to herself. Her sister was the center of attention around here. They left years ago, just kind of drifted away, here one day and gone the next. Why?"

Gus went over to the small pile of files he had carried into the house. "Look at this," he said as he handed me a green file folder, "it is a 'missing persons' filed by her mother in November 1991. There's also a runaway report from September. Seems that Lana disappeared and never came back."

"No surprise there, Gus. Everyone around here knew that the Barnes house wasn't a happy house. I know she ran off at least once or twice before when we were kids."

"You know why?"

"I've got my suspicions."

"And?"

"Well, when a kid runs away, there's usually some kind of abuse involved. The Barnes, they came and went, sometimes the girls missed school, but they never seemed to be physically injured – no bruises or black eyes. I guess, in retrospect, I'd say it was sexual abuse. The mother threw out the father at some point. But I can't know. We were kids and I had no clue. But even then, Jenny seemed so cheerful, while Lana Rae was, well–"

"You'd suspect right, Hayden. DHS report," he tossed over another file, "filed by the mother at about the same time as the second time Lana Rae ran off. The mother claimed the father had been molesting the girls. He started with the older sister, but then she got a boyfriend involved and the father backed off. I'm guessing that's when he started in on Lana Rae. Thing is, there's no indication from the mother that there was abuse going on with anyone other than the older daughter. Jenny wouldn't file any charges or testify, but the threat of going public was enough that he caved on the terms of the divorce.

"Now," Gus continued, "here's what I'm trying to figure out: Lana Rae would run off, but she always came back on her own, until the last time. And the older sister never left until she turned eighteen and made off with a boyfriend. What were those girls like?"

I told him about the inherently sexual nature of Jenny and the more retiring demeanor of her sister.

"So Lana was on the periphery? Jenny had evidently embraced sexuality as a tool, despite sexual abuse? Not entirely a surprise, I suppose. But riddle me this, Hayden: Could Lana end up in an earthen bank, dead from blunt force trauma? Who would put here there?"

"You checked on the father?"

"Dead."

Gus's phone rang. He turned back to the front window, muttering a few words before he hung up. "Well, now we know one thing for sure. Dental records are a 90 percent match for Lana Barnes. We'll be visiting again." He turned to me. "At some point you need to figure out what you know."

The rest of the evening I spent alone, staring at the ceiling above my bed, mulling the prospect of having Tara back in my life. She had offered me something – her vulnerability – and she wanted me to be her intercessor, to protect her reputation. It was a heady proposition, indeed a romantic one, to have a woman of power and position ask to serve her needs and carry her secret. It was chivalric, an old-fashioned concept of defending the fiction of virtue against the nasty reality of facts on the ground. But now it looked like her fears were taking shape.

Another call from Tara was doubtlessly forthcoming. I didn't get back to her right away about this news. But, the time had come to make checking on Salvatore part of my routine. If he was headed for trouble, he needed to have trust in me for Tara's plan to work out. For the trust to exist, Salvatore had to be used to having me as part of his life.

Chapter 21

DESPITE THIS LITTLE SIDE DRAMA, there was work to do. The next three weeks moved quickly. Mike and I traveled to Danville to attend a bid meeting for a building renovation at Centre College, and we stayed over to watch Centre play Rhodes in basketball. Much of December was taken up with planning the bid for Centre. I'd drop in on Salvatore every day or two, just to check on him, and we started playing cribbage together once a week or so, talking sports and politics and wine. Then, the Friday night before Christmas, we had a party for clients and friends out at Mike's house in the River Hills.

It was a good evening for visiting with old friends. I had not spent a lot of time socializing after I came back to the city – my first visit with family had been that Thanksgiving, and Mike and I were working six and seven days a week to get ahead on the 4th Street project. A night of wine and food and recalling old stories – old lies – ran late. I hadn't planned on staying the night, but Mike and his wife Lynn had asked, so I did. When the last of our old friends had departed, Mike and I made our way out to his pool house, a bottle of eighteen-year-old single malt in one hand, two glasses in the other.

The pool house was big, almost a guest cottage. Mike had put in an old billiard table he found at a bankrupt Portland pub that was having its contents auctioned off, and he had also bought the bar for good measure and cut it down to fit his play space. The sleeping loft upstairs was mine for the night.

I racked the balls. Mike poured the whiskey over ice, and we just shot pool and kept company. The old cues were maple, instead of the usual ash, and they had warped little over the years. Our shots were as true as the whiskey allowed.

"So Hay," Mike asked, "you happy with the project?"

"Yeah I am. The product is beautiful. I'd live in any of those houses. Are we ready to close?"

"Yep. Inspections are next week, and everything looks good. All we have to do is finish up the last house. There's a buyer."

I hadn't known that. "Great. So, what's next?"

"Well, my friend down in Danville says that our bid for the work at Centre looks promising. They like the design a lot. It is just a question of price. But, you know that they like their quality and I suspect that our main sub being an alumnus won't hurt. They can always go and shake the Boles family and the Seelbachs down for more money if need be. Hey Hay," Mike dropped the six ball in the corner, and started lining up the seven, "some gal called for you the other day, trying to find you."

"Yeah."

In goes the seven ball, to the pocket. The cue ball also drops my nine. "Tara. Just Tara."

"Yeah."

"That the same one from college? The hot little Italian girl with all that black hair?"

"Yeah. Why?"

"Seem to recall she screwed up your head pretty good. Are you getting back into that?"

"Man, I am not about to say. You know I don't like to talk about this stuff."

"C'mon, tell. You know you were always after that! I remember that one night we all got wasted over at Tina's house – remember Tina? And you went after that over in Tina's pool house? Didn't know we were all watching from up on the sun deck?"

"That wasn't Tara. That wasn't me. I never dated her in the summer. You must be thinking of Artie and Joleen. I was up on the sun deck with you guys. Remember?"

Mike chuckled to himself, "No, actually, I don't. I just remember watching. Anyhow, is this the same girl?"

"Yeah, it is. It's private."

"Private? What the hell's for private? I went into business with you, for Christ's sake, and just spent half the night watching you dirty dance and tell lies. What's private with us?"

"Mike, you know that there are some secrets we carry for each other, right?"

"Yeah. And?"

"Let's just say that if you need to know, I'll tell you, but it isn't about the business, and right now you don't need to know. She trusts me. Tara asked me to take care of something in confidence. And you know I keep my promises, as long as they don't hurt someone else."

"What is it about you and desperate women?"

"You tell me. I wish I knew."

"You always get these women who are strong but sad. Artists. Dancers. And they all drink too damned much."

"Tracy wasn't like that. She was an artist, but she was happy."

"Never met her, Hayden. The ones I get to know are the screwy drinkers who are artistic and they always make you a little crazy. You remember what you were like when you dropped Tara? Well I do. You lost your mind, didn't want to see anybody, disappeared to Gainesville and then none of us heard from you for a decade. You're not going to check out on me again, are you? Are you?"

Mike's anger and worry were visible. Where he'd slammed down his glass, scotch had splashed out onto the felt of the table.

I inhaled deep. "No, I am not. I'm through looking over horizons. Besides, she's married and rich and doesn't want me. This is me making up for a long time ago. But, my friend, I will be here."

"See that you do. We all placed a big bet on you – me, the university, the bankers, the investors – and now we're counting on you to be as talented as we all think you are."

"Okay. Mike?"

"Yeah?"

"You scratched the eight ball. Rack 'em up. It's my break."

Outside, the light snow turned heavier.

The next morning it took me an hour to make my way along the snow-covered roads to the house in Vintners Landing. On Sunday, I decided to get up and actually make mass at Saint Martin of Tours. I had not been to a mass since Tracy had been killed, but it seemed like the thing to do. The church was largely empty for the early mass, mainly just old women and a few Latino worshipers, a reminder of how much the neighborhoods around the old Catholic parishes of the 19th century had changed. As I sat through the priest's homily, I felt my phone vibrate in my pocket. It was Gus, texting: *Can you meet later today? GE*

I headed back to Cherokee County, the long way on I-71, and stopped to check on my grandmother, before I headed for the house. On the way, as I rolled through

Vintners Landing, I saw a state police cruiser and a sheriff's patrol car parked in front of the Trattoria. Salvatore was out front, talking to Gus and two uniformed officers. I thought to slow down, but instead placed a quick call to Greg Borenko.

Greg and I had grown up together too, as much adversaries as friends. He was a big, goofy kid from a divorced family, and he'd always find a way to cut into someone. I'd made a good target of his until I figured out that this was how he related to people. If you threw it back in his face, he'd respect you. He'd grown into a good politician and a good lawyer. He was at Emory Law while Tracy and I were doing houses in Atlanta, and was my only friend who ever really knew her. He'd made it big in Atlanta as a prosecutor, and then left the DA's office to join a top firm with offices in five cities. He used that as an excuse to move back home, and he just hopped flights from case to case and dealt with his partners via teleconference. He spent most of his time in federal court, and made his national name when successfully defending the Cincinnati archdiocese from a class action related to pedophile priests. He'd also take on the occasional high-profile homicide. Greg was the best, and he owed me a favor. I suspected we'd need him.

"Greg, it's Hayden. You in town? Miami? What's up down there? Trial? Look, when can you get back up here? Not until after Christmas. Shit. Call me when you get back in town, because I need to see you."

The Christmas weekend passed without event. I had gotten up early Christmas morning and drove up to my grandmother's to start breakfast for all the family that would show up at eleven. We cooked and talked politics, making time go slow. There would be almost fifty at the house that morning. My college-age cousins and a cousin in the Navy had made it home, and the whole scene from Thanksgiving would play out again, but this time with secret Santa gifts and two meals instead of one – brunch and supper. Nothing caught fire, so Uncle Caleb and I spent the afternoon in the garage rebuilding the top of a short block Chevy and talking football. Others came and went, but we just stayed in the garage until Christmas supper, enjoying the sweet smell of the kerosene furnace as big wet snow fell to the ground outside.

Chapter 22

THE COWBELL CLANGED as I came through the door of the Trattoria. No one was at the counter out front. "Salvatore! Salvatore! You in here?"

"Come in back Hayden. Just fixing some supper. Care to stay?"

"Absolutely. Man, that smells great. What is it?"

"*Capretto Ripieno al Forno* – roast kid – and *caponata* – you know eggplant and olive antipasto. I've got to do books tonight, start getting ready for tax time. So I figured I'd eat well."

Salvatore and I were by now in the habit of visiting every evening, at least for a few minutes, sometimes for an hour or so over supper. He'd cook, or sometimes I'd bring in barbeque from the city, and then we'd chat about the weather or business or politics. He still opened for dinner on weekends, so we'd just have coffee and talk. Sometimes, we'd talk family. Or we'd play cribbage, if the traffic at the counter was light.

"I'm not sure if I can keep it going, Hayden."

"Why? Is the Trattoria losing money?"

"Not so much, but the work is getting harder and harder. Hayden, I worked in this place six days a week for forty years. All the family that kept me here is gone. Mother's in Alabama half the year with Lenore, Mama is gone, Danny's dead. I never see Tara. It makes money, but I feel like the world is driving by sometimes."

"Salvatore," I paused, spearing another *chianima* steak from the platter, "what would you do if you were not here. Where would you go?"

"Go? Hayden, I can't rightly tell you that. Except for a year at college, this is the only place I know. I suppose somewhere warm. Someplace with pretty women."

"Then go."

Salvatore smiled his big smile, looking down at the plate, working his antipasto. "Aw Hay, you know I can't go. Old man like me. I gotta stay here and see this thing through. Mama built the business and I've got to keep it going. I've got customers, they've come here for decades."

"Why? Salvatore, the land alone is worth a fortune. The business has value – you could sell it. You've got great frontage on the crest of a hill on the highway headed to the lake. Some developer would pay you well for this land. Then you can go off."

"I wouldn't know where to go."

"Tara thinks you should go."

He dropped the fork, and got up and walked over to the sink. He placed his hands on the counter, back to me, looking down.

"You've talked to Tara?"

"Yes I have. She's worried Salvatore. She's worried about you."

"She'd have no call to worry about me. She's a sweet girl, but she was wild, like Danny, like Lenore. Where is she, anyway?"

"She's here in town Salvatore. She lives in a big house on the river, and she's a successful businesswoman. Tara built a life, got away from Vintners Landing. She wants you to do the same."

"Why? I've got no cause to leave."

"I think you do."

Salvatore turned, and stared at me. "You do? You don't even know me anymore. You never did. You were a kid."

"I know the police were talking to you. Four weeks ago, out front after you'd closed."

"Someone broke into the storeroom."

"I don't believe you Salvatore. You know that body they found under the trestle last month? Well, she's Lana Rae Barnes."

Salvatore stared at me, blankly. A minute. Two.

"I can help you, Salvatore. You want to leave, you can leave and no one will know the wiser. Tara says she'll help you. You just let me know."

The front bell clattered. Salvatore grabbed his apron and headed out front.

"Be right with you!" Then he turned to me. "You don't know what the hell you're talking about. And neither does Tara. You better get home."

I left.

Chapter 23

DOUG AND ORLEY AND I HEADED OUT deer hunting the next day. Winter means doe days back home, but we were looking for a buck. We stayed away for three days, celebrating New Year's in a deer stand with a bottle of Early Times. We each bagged our bucks on the third day and headed home. The next night, January 3, I'd meet with Greg and start trying to figure out what to do about Salvatore if the police came back.

Greg had called. He was flying in from Florida, and he said he'd take a taxi to meet me at the River King.

The River King was a joint we used to hang out at on college breaks, an old blues club that had sprung up along with Dave's Palm Room as a 'destination venue' for quality music in Louisville. It had started out in the 1920s as a juke joint, a place traveling jazz and R&B performers would hit headed South after touring the Midwest, or for after-hours fun when they played the nearby Palm Room. The rich power of the local sound came from poverty and the closeness of segregation, and also from a historic black high school that had placed a premium on artistic achievement. Later, touring white entertainers found the place on the word of Louis Armstrong. Then the college kids started making their way to the River King, and the cocaine dealers were soon to follow.

I got to the River King at about ten, still early enough to grab a table. The place was smoky, but the softened walls and the wall-to-wall crowd of gyrating bodies absorbed a lot of the noise. It was intimate and anonymous. The main act that night was a jazz/hip-hop fusion group out of Lafayette, Louisiana. I ordered a beer and settled back to watch the room. A couple of the working girls came by to make small talk, but paying for company wasn't what I had in mind.

About eleven, Greg showed up. He hadn't changed much since we had known each other in school – the earring and the ponytail were new, but otherwise he still looked like a kid from suburbs.

"Hayden!" We exchanged the manly hug of old friends and athletes. The fusion band blazed away in the corner of the bar as the college kids and the locals dirty danced and shouted. "I thought I'd never find this place! I hadn't been here in years. How excellent! You got dates for us too?"

"You never come down here?"

"Not so much. I mainly just hang out at that place by the marina near Harrod's Creek, hitting the divorcees. I figure if they lived that long and look that good, they're clean. Man, look at the tail tonight!"

The server made her way over. "Two more of those," Greg indicated my beer, "man, what a flight. Storms from Miami all the way up here. You'd think that this late in the season we'd get a break."

We kept up the small talk for a few more minutes. His most recent divorce. My hiding in Hungary. Finally came the time to discuss business.

"I guess you want to know why you're here, Greg."

"Well, the clock started running the moment I got on the plane, so my curiosity can wait if you want. It isn't my money."

"Well, you remember Tara?"

Greg paused for a moment of fake reflection. "You went out with her in college, right? I vaguely remember. Vaguely. The leggy Italian girl, right? Did I meet her?"

"Yeah, that's the one, and no you never met her. You'd remember her. Anyhow, her brothers were both friends of mine. One of them was killed when I was in high school.

Anyhow, the other brother, Salvatore, he's landed in trouble and he needs a good lawyer."

"She's Danny's sister? Damn. So how'd you get involved? You back in there?"

I glared back.

"Hey, no reason to get pissed, Hayden! She's all you talked about for the year we lived together. Seriously, why are you involved? Plenty of good lawyers up here. Why call me up from Miami?"

The beers arrived. "Tara got in touch with me because Salvatore was questioned by the police. There's a body, dead girl, and they think he is involved in her death. I don't have enough details of the investigation to be sure, but from what I do know he needs counsel." I had to keep my lies, for my own sake and also for Greg's. He wasn't my counsel.

"And?"

"And he has been refusing to get a lawyer and Tara asked me to find someone good. Because he has been questioned without counsel, because he has refused to get counsel, it'll be messy. They have not charged him yet, but it is coming. Look, Greg, the reason I called is because of a talk we had a long time ago, right after you went to the DeKalb County public defender's office. Remember how you picked clients?"

"I only took guilty clients because, as a PD, you're probably going to lose anyway. So successfully defending a client you know is guilty is the greatest test of a defense lawyer. If you can get a guilty man off you can probably win any trial. Are you sure he's guilty?"

"He looks guilty as hell, but I'm sure he didn't do it." I laid out for him the story in an hour over two more beers.

"Tara has money. She'll take care of the bills. Will you meet with him?"

"No time like the present. I'll get the check. You get your car."

Another snow had started to fall, and it was a wet snow that made the pavement slick and unpredictable. A wreck on I-64 at Blankenbaker Lane closed the highway, so we dropped onto U.S. 60 and took it out to Shelbyville then took the old National Highway to Cherokee County. I had to take it slow once we left the interstate, and by the time we made it out to Vintners Landing, a good six inches coated the road as the snow changed over to an icy sleet. As we inched along the winding two-lane, my old Mustang loudly protested the cold weather. The branches of the old oaks that draped over the road started to bough under the weight of the ice and snow.

We came into Vintners Landing from the south, passed through town and headed for the intersection of 14 and 44. As I made the turn in the road by Brashear's grocery, the light of blue flashers lit the sky. Four patrol cars were parked in the front lot, and a pair of deputies milled about, bracing against the cold. Pulling into the parking lot, I saw the lights on inside the old store. It was almost two in the morning, long after closing time.

As we got out of the car, one of the deputies came over. "Sir! There's nothing of interest here! Please return to your car and move on!"

Greg was about to make his protest when the old storm door swung open, the cowbell clattering. Gus Ellis and another deputy we went to school with, Danny Hoage, came out, escorting Salvatore. He was dressed, as always, in his slacks and a flannel shirt, everything perfectly pressed in place. His face was impassionate, featureless, his arms cuffed behind his back. He did not make eye contact with any of us as they took him toward a waiting unmarked car.

Gus saw me. "Hayden, whatever you are doing here, you'd better just step back and move on while I do my job!"

"Officer," Greg interrupted, "I –"

"Detective. Detective Deputy Ellis. And who the hell are you?"

Greg stole a quick glance toward me, and I quickly nodded.

"Detective Ellis, I'm Greg Borenko, Salvatore Lichten's lawyer. I trust that you have not been questioning my client without benefit of counsel, that you advised him of his rights. Now," Greg continued, "where are you taking my client?"

Gus put his hands on his hips and looked at the ground. Then he looked up. "Counselor, your client is under arrest for murder. You can see him up at central holding at the jail. Arraignment court is at nine, so you've got time to go get your fancy suit. Rollin," he turned to me, and pulled me aside "we need to talk."

Greg leaned into Salvatore, now in the back of the car, and muttered something. Salvatore sat, stone-faced. I turned back to Gus. "What?"

"I think you are now material to this case. Please be in my office, noon tomorrow."

"We'll see. Call my lawyer."

Ellis left in the unmarked patrol car. We followed them back to Carritherston, and I called Tara to wake her up and have her meet us at the courthouse. No answer, so I left an ambiguous message. I'd call again later. Before we left, I pulled shut the door to the Trattoria, turning over the "Closed" sign and testing the lock.

We drove along in silence, the snow piling heavy on the trees. As we drew close to town, Greg said, "Look, just in case, you better get a lawyer too. If they want to question you, I cannot represent your interests. I may have to question you or cross-examine you before this is over. Salvatore is my client. It is possible, from what you told me, that I may have to break part of a story you may tell. Can our friendship handle that?"

"Yes."

Once we got downtown, I dropped Greg at the courthouse. Greg headed into the sheriff's office and started working over the undersheriff to get to Salvatore. I slept in the car, waiting for Greg to come back.

At about four in the morning I gave up on waiting and went in to find out what was going on. Greg was with Salvatore. They'd be awhile, probably staying together until the arraignment hearing at nine.

You better get a lawyer.

Greg was right. I went ahead and called Doug. He was still at the office in Carritherston, working all night through a divorce deposition. He had done his fair share of homicides as an assistant DA a few years back. I told him what went down with Salvatore.

Silence.

I prompted Doug for an answer. "Hayden, I'll meet you for coffee before we see Gus. We'll have to play a lot of it by ear."

Doug hung up. I placed another call. Since Greg was occupied with Salvatore, who was about to be charged with murder, I knew that I needed to call Tara again.

"Hayden," she whispered, "I can't have you calling when Daemon is in the house! Especially in the middle of the night. I had to dance all 'round the message on the machine when we came in."

"Listen to me. So sorry to have called that way, but I figured you'd want to know that Salvatore was in jail. I need to bail him out."

"Jail! When?"

"Sheriff picked him up in Vintners Landing about three hours ago. Greg – the lawyer I told you about – Greg is with him. We were there when he was arrested, but I have no idea what he said or did. We need to meet."

"I can't come to the courthouse. You know I can't do that."

"I know. Look, arraignment is at nine. In a case like this, where he didn't flee and he has ties to the community, figure that the bond will be a half-million. Greg will try for OR – own recognizance – but figure on having to either post property or a bond."

Tara paused at the other end of the phone. "What am I going to do? I can get the cash, but I cannot be involved."

"Meet me at the Castleburger on Mount Eden Road. It's right off of I-64 – there's no reason you wouldn't be down there early on a Thursday morning, especially if you had to go to Lexington. You'll see my old Mustang out front. Park and I'll follow you in."

"What time?

"Seven-thirty."

Why, I asked myself, *why am I involving myself in this mess?*

I parked beside the Castleburger and settled in for a nap. Drunken high school kids rolled through the drive-through, loading up on greasy onion burgers and soggy fries. At about 5:30, a state police trooper rapped on my window with his flashlight – Sam Diffee, an old friend of Dad's. He bought my story that I had worked late at the jobsite on Fourth and that I was waiting on a sub-contractor. I went in at six and bought a coffee, and settled back into the car to wait. The gray dawn meant more snow to come.

Tara's little Audi rolled into the parking lot at 7:30. She was dressed down – hair up, sunglasses, jogging suit – but still looked out of place in this land of grease populated with laborers, drunks, and other forms of hangers-on. She went in to the counter and ordered something; I followed her in, and got in line behind her and ordered four burgers and another coffee. We made the small talk of casual acquaintances and then sat at the little window counter looking out toward the parking lot.

"Tara, first things first – if I am supposed to act as your agent, I have to know how to get hold of you – immediately. I can't dance around Daemon like we're having some kind of affair. You have to find a way to, to communicate efficiently. Do you have a cell?"

She gave me the number. "Call. You can use your name, but make it in the context of the business. Better yet, text. I'll tell him we're thinking about hiring you to do a store for us or something. Now, what about Salvatore?"

"I've been thinking about that, and I think I have an idea. I can post the bond, but I'll need financial cover."

"How?"

"I can post the bond using the line of credit I have on one of my properties. Ten percent of the bond won't be more than $100,000, and I know a bondsman who will cover that bond. Salvatore's no flight risk. You will need to cut me a check this week, a retainer for services in the same amount. No financial risk for me and my partner, no paper trail for you. And Salvatore doesn't spend time in jail. The alternative is that he puts up the restaurant for surety."

"What if he does walk?"

"If he puts up the Trattoria, he loses it. And he probably gets caught. If I post the bond, well –"

"Yes?"

"Then you better come up with a hell of a lot of work for me and my business partner."

"Done. And Hayden –"

"Yes," I was up and about to head for the door.

"Thank you." A tear made its way down her cheek from under the sunglasses.

I nodded and left, because I wanted to be out of her reach. Besides, I had an hour to arrange with my bank in Atlanta to advance the money for the bond.

Chapter 24

THE ARRAIGNMENT HEARING WENT SMOOTHLY enough. Greg entered a not-guilty plea for Salvatore, and the judge set bond at a half-million dollars. I offered up the bond, acquired through a bondsman who accepted the house in New Orleans as collateral. An hour later, a half-million dollars was wired into my account in Atlanta. A retainer agreement arrived at the brownstone from Tara's East End, LLC, for architectural and planning services.

As Greg and Salvatore walked out of the courthouse in Carritherston, I motioned Salvatore over to the truck I'd brought from the job site and told him to get in back. No press yet, which was good. Gus promised Greg a low-profile arraignment because he was cooperative in the arrest. But this story wouldn't stay quiet any longer. Greg and I leaned on the hood of the truck.

"Cigarette?" He motioned with the pack.

"Yeah." I grabbed one of the Camels and he lit us up.

"So," Greg said to the wind, "this is a real winner, Hayden. A client who won't talk, forensics link him to the body, time and place link him to the victim, pattern of prior behavior and potential witnesses who saw him with her often before she was killed. This is going to break a winning streak I've got going. We're even now, understood?"

"Yeah. We're even. So what do we do now?"

"Well, here's like anywhere. The media feeding frenzy will start with the noon news. The odds are, there will be an Internet story within ten minutes at the *Courier*, and then it hits the AP, and then the TV stations run it. His occupation brings him into frequent contact with the public, and he's not going to be safe. We need to find a safe place to squirrel him away, maybe even hire a security firm to protect him. He'll have to padlock the Trattoria for a while, and someone will need to watch it too."

"So Greg, where do we keep him?"

"Been turning that over in my head too. One of my partners has a cabin on Greene River – secluded, quiet, and easy to defend this time of year. I get a couple of Pinkertons out there to watch over him, maybe ask the police to deputize them so that they don't think Salvatore's a flight risk. Basically we put him in protective custody. Otherwise, someone will try to kill him."

"You think?"

"This county? A guy who killed a young girl, hid it like that? Sex crime? Hell yes, some red neck with a daughter will think to take justice in his own hands. The nuts come out of the woods for this kind of case."

"Send me the bills."

We climbed in the pickup. "Salvatore."

He looked up at my eyes in the rear view mirror.

"Salvatore?"

"Yes Mr. Borenko?"

"Salvatore, we're going to take you home and get some things, and then we're going to take you to a safe house out of town."

"What about the restaurant?"

"Hayden and I will take care of the Trattoria. You need to just go rest. We'll start on a defense in a few days."

Chapter 25

THE MEDIA FRENZY WAS EVERYTHING Greg had expected. All five local news stations did stand-ups in front of the Trattoria, by the train trestle, in front of the courthouse.

They had photos of Lana Rae from our high school yearbook, photos from a *Today's Living* magazine piece on Salvatore's Trattoria. They ran down Jenny and got an interview with her, talking about how her sister disappeared and what a shame it was that such a good Christian girl should meet such a horrible end. The media contacted me repeatedly, trying to get me on tape talking about why I posted bond. I released a statement through Doug, as the family lawyer, explaining the close ties of our families and how I just couldn't let Salvatore languish in jail until his trial date.

The coverage was getting out of hand. Someone in the police department or the commonwealth attorney's office was leaking details of the case, details that really needed to wait for a jury to be called and seated. The trial in the media had begun. A local online muckracking publication started a blog dedicated to the killing. Soon, the Internet crazies were speculating about "other bodies" and making Salvatore out to be a serial killer. Mike was very upset over the publicity – TV cameras showed up at the office and down at the Fourth Street job site. But, within about ten days, the cameras and the reporters went away.

Then there was no new information. Sheriff Lowery clamped down on his department. Doug called a judge who Papaw had trained as a rookie cop, and His Honor sent a quiet message to the commonwealth attorney's office for the 53rd judicial circuit to can the chatter on the Lichten case.

They treated me as one of their own – the thin blue line extended itself.

Tara had fled to the Bahamas and Daemon's boat to ride out the storm. The media had not put her together with the Salvatore, at least not yet. Lenore and Angina came back from Mobile to attend to affairs and support him. I had one of Greg's associates pick them up and get them to Greene River – I needed to tend my own garden. I acted as Tara's agent, I'd visit with Salvatore, but I had other commitments.

IV: A Gentleman Can Live Through Anything

Chapter 26

CHRISTMAS WAS OVER. THE NEW YEAR was rung in. The major party season was over until the beginning of the spring meets, and even though there were social events for the company, I was at work.

I checked on Salvatore every few days, but he was quiet, not sure who to trust. Mainly, I saw to his needs through the lawyers, and tried to move on with the rest of my life. We had finished all of the houses but one and had closing on all of them at the end of January. The last house was still underway, behind schedule. The weather had been slowing down material deliveries, and Mike was busy negotiating the deal to start on the new lofts downtown. I was working nights to finish the carpentry work so we could make the end of January closing. It was good to be working with wood again, if only to take a break from being sociable.

December had been demanding at work, and the social swirl of the holidays had worn me down. Single, straight and thirty-three, I was tailor-made for the eighth seat at any dinner party. Every fix-up possible came my way, from old high school classmates to friends of family and friends of friends and even friends of our banker. I went on them all, for a while, but I had settled into a social habit of Mike and Lynn, Doug, a few other old friends. There is such a thing as too many parties, and when family and friends are determined to fix you up, the invitations come fast and furious.

But, for tonight, no social obligations were to be met. Greg was busy trying to walk Salvatore through the preparation for the discovery phase of his prosecution, working up motions, lining up experts, even preparing a mental incompetence defense. There was no use in my being around, so I just kept the checks flowing and texted Tara when something needed her attention.

It was just me and the finish carpentry work on the third-floor study of the last brownstone. The new shelving was in place, so all I had left to do was wainscoting and crown molding for the study, and some trim work in the guest bedroom. It was relatively warm out – fifties – so I threw open the casement windows and let the sounds of the city drift through the house. Two blocks over, the faint din of a stereo drifted through the air, as the students at the university celebrated a win over Georgetown with a street party over on Confederate Boulevard. Out on the street, cars drove back and forth, some slowing to eyeball the renovation work, others headed out to parties or home from shopping.

But I was lost in wood, content with my miter chop saw and my nail gun, the sound of the air compressor downstairs drowning out the sounds of the streets. Measure. Mark. Measure again. Cut. After an hour I hit my stride. By eleven the study and the guest room were finished, and ready for staining and sealing. I was beat, covered in sawdust, and ready for a break. I headed down to the kitchen and found a cold one, and slumped against the wall to enjoy the end of the day.

"Hi. Don't get up."

I looked up to see Tara standing in the door.

"Couldn't if I wanted to."

"Well, that's a fine reception for a lady, Mister Doctor Rollin. Are you at least going to offer a lady a drink?"

"Depends. Looks like you've got a head start on me."

"Oh, Daemon had some horse breeder thing that I dropped in on. Mimosas with Grey Goose enhancements are a lovely way to survive that horsey set. I learned that in Staadt."

"Touché. But did I ever drink with you that we didn't end up in bed? Think you can control yourself?"

"You're cute, but you're not all that irresistible, Hayden Rollin."

"Hah! Fair enough. Pull up a piece of floor. It's all I've got to offer you. Here," I tossed her a cold beer, "house brands only."

She slumped down the wall beside me, her fox fur fluffing away the sawdust on the floor.

We sat there for five minutes, staring out the French doors into the rear courtyard. No words passed between us, only bottles.

"Another one, Tah-Rah?"

"Sure."

Another round, another five minutes, no more words. After a half hour we had finished all the beer and the bottle of whiskey in the cooler. We were still sitting on the floor, nicely drunk, still not talking. Tara was building a pyramid with the empties, while I contemplated whether or not to go on a real bender.

"So," I said, "What, exactly, brought you down here from the stylish set up there in Prospect? Get tired of the Bahamas? I figured you'd have some vital charitable work to do for Africa in advance of the tax-write-off giving season. Or did you just drop in to check on the help?"

"You, you Hayden Rollin, you are an arrogant, arrogant carpenter. Look around you! You just blow into town, no one's seen you in a dozen years, you blow into the town, and, and you –"

"Blow into town. Yeah. Got that – ouch! Christ, those heels hurt!"

"You deserved that, you. You blow into town, a dozen years, and you just drop into renovating eight beautiful houses. No one's seen you for years, you ignore your family, forget your friends, and here you are. 'Oh, I just thought I'd drop into everyone's life from Vienna –'"

"Budapest."

"Wherever. Europe, somewhere exotic. You just drop in and everyone's life is turned upside down. Before you got in town, I didn't have to think about any of this, of this, well, oh. Any of this ... stuff with Salvatore and all of that crap from my grandmother's family. You can't imagine what it was like in that house."

She was rolling. I should have left it alone.

"Oh for Christ's sake, Tara, everyone has a life that sucks sometimes. Every family is nuts."

"No, no, this was different. So very different. There was no joy in that house, none at all. Everyday, in everyway, everyone was trying to hold on to what they had, afraid that someone might take something from them. You had to act a particular way, look a particular way, dress a particular way. Mama ruled that house, and she tormented everyone on down the line with her disappointment and her demands."

"Tara, I hate to tell you this, but, well, everyone knew that –"

"No, no, no! Do not tell me that, because you can't know."

"Why not?"

"Because," she started, and then the tears came. "Because you could leave. You didn't have to stay through the yelling arguments between Mama and Miss Angina, Mama and Salvatore, Salvatore and Miss Angina. Or, they'd all get started, and get going on each other. And it would all come out, especially if Mother – Miss Angina – had been drinking. Every disappointment you ever caused would be visited on you, over, and over, and over. It was worse than a beating, worse than, than –" She collapsed into a gasping sob.

"Oh, Tara, I am so sorry." She had slumped over on me, holding on and sobbing quietly into her coat. I tried to talk, but she just shushed me with her hand.

"Hayden, be quiet. Don't talk."

"One question?"

"One."

"Why did you ever come here?"

"I, I – oh shut up!" And she kissed me, hard, forcefully, and pushed me down onto the floor, her fox sweeping over us both, obliterating the light and scattering the empty cans and sawdust across the floor.

Dawn's light has a noise.

"*Hayden.*"

"Huh?"

"*Hayden.*"

"Oh, hey Mike. What's up?"

He pressed a finger to his lips. "*Shhh. I didn't want to wake up your, ah, company.*" Mike pointed to my left, where Tara was sleeping, dead to the world and wrapped in her fox. "*Looks like old times there, son.*"

"Oh-h-h. Ow. Hand me my jeans. Okay, thanks. Look, Mike, is anyone else here?"

"*Not yet. It's only about seven.*"

"Good. Do me a favor," I groped around, looking for Tara's key, and then handed them to him. "Go out front and look for the Audi that fits this key, and move it around into the alley. And give me five minutes."

Tara didn't make a sound as I scooped her up in her fox and carried her up to the second floor bedroom. It was still furnished from when I was living in the house; I tucked her away in the bed and laid the fox at the foot of the bed, and then went and gathered her clothes and clutch and brought them upstairs. As I closed the door, I heard Mike downstairs, sending off the two guys who did our finish work.

"Mike, you didn't give them the day off?"

"No. I rushed them off to get some materials we need to finish up. We're on a deadline, and I can't give up labor for even one day and keep the money burn under control. So," Mike grabbed the back of my neck as we walked out to the sidewalk, "you want to explain why I find you naked, on the floor, with a naked and attractive client?"

"Because I'm a whore?"

"Yep, because you're a whore, Hayden. You get a cookie. Now what happened? I need to know if Lynn should avoid inviting you guys to the same parties. Get a shirt on and let me take you for a cup of coffee. We need to talk about the downtown project. I need to know if you're sticking around or not."

"Tell Lynn her Derby Week party list is fine. It needn't change. Oh, Christ," the hangover announced itself, "Can we do this later, Mike? I really ought to be here when she wakes up."

"Now there's a change for you, staying until dawn. Good man. Stick around. Don't come waking me up to help you make your escape. Nice change for you, I'll say. We'll get together for lunch. Eleven o'clock good?"

"Good."

"Later. You dog."

Mike walked off to his Porsche, leaving me staring into the white haze of the morning sun. The silver catering break truck came rolling by. I flagged them down and got two large coffees and a few of donuts, and took them back upstairs to check on Tara. She was still sound asleep, her long black hair undone and lying across the pillows, her bare shoulders just visible beneath the down comforter. Her face was content, remarkably unlined and unblemished despite the stresses she carried.

I sat in the overstuffed chair in the corner for an hour, just watching her sleep. The passion and satisfaction with the night before cut through the beery fog of my brain. She had been vicious, like the last time we had been together. And, back then, that was enough.

But, I also felt a sense of guilt, and of loss. Seeing Tara there, recalling the night before, drove home to me that Tracy was gone and she would not be back. There would never be any substitute for the easy love I had enjoyed with her, for her.

"Oh. Oh, oh. Oh fuck. Hayden." Tara buried her head in the pillows.

"That was earlier. 'Good morning Hayden' is the new call sign."

"Be nice. Hayden. Oh God. Where are we?"

"Upstairs. The brownstone on Fourth." I walked over to the bed and sat on the edge. "Coffee?"

"Yes." Tara turned over and sat up in bed, pulling the covers up around her. "Oh God, that is truly awful coffee. Where'd you get it?"

"Break truck. These are the instant crystals you can get on wheels. May I now speak?"

She smiled the tiniest smile. "Yes."

"Why *did* you ever come here?"

"Because I was lonely, and you are different and honest. I feel safe with you and I needed to take away the loneliness."

Stifling a smart remark, I said nothing. I doubt she thought of what she did as using me. I was a willing accomplice. Better to let it go.

"What happened?"

"Hayden, it's all such a mess. Daemon and I, we hardly seem to see each other. He was so virile and strong when we first got together, but he's turning into an old man, more interested in the horses than anything else. I don't know if he has the ability to be jealous."

"So it's about sex?"

"No. It's about attention, about someone listening and paying attention and wanting to actually listen, and understand. Hayden, his solution to everything anymore is to write a check and get away from the problem as soon as possible. I've got the business and I've got 'friends,' such as they are – a bunch of chattering country-club trophies – but I don't have any intimacy anymore. I don't know if I can trust anyone."

"With all due respect, dear Tara, doesn't that sound like your solution too? Write a check, get away? Salvatore asks after you, he wants to see you. So, you send me with a lawyer and a check."

Silence greeted my analysis.

"Well, until you know who to trust, trust me. It'll be hard, but it'll have to be enough. Now," I stood up, "the work crew won't be back for an hour. Your car is in the alley, so duck out the back. Two days. Lunch at that bistro you like, the one on Bardstown Road. I'll be at a table in the back. We'll talk then. Okay?"

"Okay." She kissed my cheek. "Now get out of here so I can get decent."

She didn't show for lunch, and she wasn't returning my text messages. I drove down to Greene River and made dinner with Salvatore. I didn't say anything about Tara, or whether I'd seen here. She'd make her presence known eventually.

"Hayden, this isn't half bad." Salvatore sampled my effort at Italian cuisine. "I didn't know you could make *strozzapreti* with black truffles. These are delicious. And this wine, a nice pinot. Was it in the cellar?"

"Yes, I hope you don't mind, but I went into your stores to make this. My late wife Tracy, she loved to cook. There was a little Italian bistro around the corner from our place in New Orleans, La Bella Dona. The chef there loved Tracy's art, and they'd swap out paintings for lessons. She taught me a couple of his recipes."

"He was from central Italy?"

"Apennine hills. I also make a mean seafood tripe. Maybe you let me cook down at the Trattoria one night?"

Salvatore demurred a moment. "Maybe. You're a good boy, Hayden, always were. We'll see. I must first get through this."

"Sal?"

"Yes, Hayden?"

"Why won't you talk? Talk to the police, or the commonwealth's attorney, or your lawyer? It's like you want to kill yourself."

Salvatore paused a moment. "Open another bottle of wine, Hayden. Let's go on the deck and maybe I can explain this to you. But not in here." He motioned over his shoulder where his older sister and mother drowsed on the sofa of the cabin's great room.

"Very well." I pulled the last bottle of Schug 2005 from the box I'd brought from the Trattoria, and we headed out into the cool, dark night.

"Mind if I smoke, Sal?"

"Actually, yes. I never liked that habit."

I put away my pack, and uncorked the wine instead.

"So why won't you tell what actually happened? Or come clean? Did you do this thing, Salvatore?"

Salvatore turned, and looked me straight in the eye. "Hayden, you must believe me, whatever things I may have done in my life, I did not kill that girl. I have never killed a human being in my life."

"Then say so!" My voice went up in exasperation. "None of us understand why you won't talk. Greg, Doug, Tara, none of us. Why can't you even say that much to the authorities?"

"If I speak to them, I have to do so under oath. I cannot say that I did not kill that girl under oath."

"Why not? If you're innocent, what is the problem?"

"No one is innocent, Hayden. At best we are not guilty, but only newborn children are innocent. No, no, no one is innocent, and even though I didn't kill Lana, it doesn't mean I am innocent in her death."

"You know who killed her, don't you?" I pressed. He looked away. "You do! Oh Christ, you know! God damn it, Salvatore, you can't go to the chair for another man! Scream your innocence!"

"Hayden!" Salvatore's face flushed with anger. "Don't you think I would if I could? I can say this here, now, because there's no oath, there's no consequence. Once I put my hand on that Bible and take an oath to God to tell the truth, I have to tell the whole truth. I can profess my innocence, but I cannot turn my finger toward the man who did this awful thing. Under oath, the state controls me, controls what I get to say. If asked a question, one must answer truthfully. Omission through silence is a bad as a lie, and I will either have to lie before God or break another vow. So, silence is my only option." His eyes welled. He had the resigned look of a man who knew he would soon die.

"Salvatore, you have to come forward and defend yourself. No man should pay for the sins of another."

"We all pay for the sins of others, Hayden. That's my life."

I stayed until about eleven, then drove home to Vintners Landing. When I got back to the farm, there was an email message from Doug. Gus wanted to see us down at sheriff's office, next morning.

I was ready for this episode to end, so I could get back to my life. Salvatore was proving to be impossible. Tara was proving to be more fickle than I remembered. So, of course, I could not get her out of my mind.

But, for the first time in years, my mind was not preoccupied with the ghost of Tracy.

Chapter 27

"HAYDEN, THANKS FOR COMING IN."

"Gus."

Gus walked back around behind the conference table and sat down. He motioned us to chairs. "So," he started, "who is the suit?"

"Doug Cuinard. I'm Hayden's cousin. I'm also his lawyer."

Gus looked Doug up and down, and glanced at his notes. "You're Cuinard? More family. Lawyer? You a Dixon or a Rollin?"

"A Dixon." Doug eyed him back. "Does it matter?"

"Nope. Just trying to figure out how many of you are floating around here. Now, Hayden, first of all, let me tell you off the bat that you are not a person of interest in this investigation. Never were. But I think I owe you an explanation of where we are. And, I think you owe me the consideration of helping fill in some gaps. Can you do that?"

"We'll see. Unzip and show me yours and we'll see, Gus."

"Counselor," he directed his attention to Doug, "can I count on your discretion as an officer of the court?"

Doug nodded his assent.

"Here's what I've got, Hayden. I've got a dead body that is Lana Rae Barnes, a seventeen-year-old woman who was killed about seventeen years ago. The last reported sighting of her was in 1991, when her parents filed a missing persons report on her. I've got evidence that ties Salvatore Lichten to her death. Physical evidence at the crime scene matches his. More specifically, I've got a bloody thumb print that is a nine-point match to his prints from the Kentucky driver license data base. The knife that killed her was in the back of the storage building at the grocery. That was enough to bring him in and put him under arrest. We're in the process of gathering other evidence to compare to the physical evidence preserved at the site."

"Gus," Doug observed, "it sounds like you've got your case. Why drag Hayden down here?"

"Counselor, I'm curious about a couple of things. First of all, why did you go out and get a lawyer for Salvatore Lichten? Second, and more important, why would this man kill Lana Rae?"

"And you think I can answer those questions?" My blood pressure was up. "Why should I answer these questions? Why I retained him a lawyer is none of your damned business. He's entitled to counsel. And, if I'm paying for his lawyer, why would I answer your questions?"

Gus slumped in his chair. "Look, man, one cop to another – I need to figure this one out. Your boy Salvatore's never committed a crime, but he looks awfully funny on paper. In fact, he looks a hell of a lot like a serial killer. We've got what we need to put him away. Now, reason I bring this up is that this killing doesn't fit a serial killer profile. No other bodies, no trademark ritual to the execution. But, maybe it is possible. Maybe we found just the first link in a chain of victims."

"Why do you say that, Gus?" Now he had me curious. Doug and I both hunched forward.

"I did a little checking. From about 1982 to 1991, there were periodic animal mutilations out there in your part of the county. Dogs and cats found hanged or burned or both. They usually took place on the weekends, or sometimes weekdays during the summer. Now, sometimes a killer with issues with women starts with animals. Usually they're kids, but my psychologist says that sometimes you'll find an adult serial killer starting out the same way."

"That's it?"

"There's also a lot of arson. About half-a-dozen houses and several barns and sheds burned out there from about '82 to '91. Then, all of a sudden, after November '91, nothing. No house fire or shed fire that was concluded to be arson."

I turned to Doug and said, "Arson is also considered a potential precursor to serial killer behavior. So you think Salvatore was doing all this, Gus?"

"Hayden, I'm just sayin' – single man, lives at home with his mother, has no contact with women outside of work or his family, flirts with young women, never dates. You tell me – he fits the profile."

"For what?" Doug chuckled. "A gay man? C'mon, detective."

Gus ignored Doug. "Now, one thing I can't establish yet is a timeline. Now when is the last time you remember seeing Lana Rae Barnes?"

"Why ask me?"

"Because Jenny Barnes said I should," Gus looked at Doug, "she said I should ask *both* of you, counselor. And some guy named Mike."

I looked at Doug. He nodded back. "Deal. Doug, you want to tell the story, or shall I?"

"I'm just the lawyer here, baby. You tell the story, and I'll tell you when to shut up. Gus, this conversation is deep background. Let's take a walk and then we can talk."

"Mr. Cuinard, I don't think you were listening. She said talk to both of you. You can't be the lawyer."

"Then we're not talking."

Gus deflated a bit. Placing his hands on the table, he looked at us both. "Look, I need to figure this damned thing out. I don't think your boy did it, but the evidence keeps pointing at him. Tell me your story, deep background, and maybe I can figure out what we're all missing."

"Not here," Doug said. "And not now. And not in this jurisdiction."

Gus looked at the file, looked at his hands. "Fine. I just need to figure out the roadmap. Name your place."

"You like oysters, Gus?"

"No, I hate them."

"Great. We'll be at Mazzoni's by Bowman Field in Louisville. One o'clock."

Mazzoni's had opened down by the stockyards a hundred years ago, offering a free "rolled" oyster with a beer to thirsty patrons. Rolled oysters are Chesapeake oysters, rolled in a doughy batter and deep-fried. The original restaurant was long gone, but part of the original bar stood in the location across from the Bowman Field, frequented by hungry professionals on the lunch hour, looking for fried seafood and a cold drink. It was forty minutes from Carritherston, an hour by the commuter train that stopped in Saint Matthews on the way downtown. It was a good place for dead man's talk.

Doug got there first, taking a table around the side of the bar. The place was noisy as always, with the clatter of dishes and the call of orders barking from the waitresses to the fryers in back. I stood over at the bar, sipping a cold beer. When Gus came in, Doug motioned him over. A couple of minutes later, Doug buzzed my phone once. I paid for the beer and joined them.

"I hate this place," Gus muttered. "Oysters. Fried greasy oily crap."

"Then have the fish, on rye. Hey honey!" The waitress came over for our order. Doug took charge. "Plate of rolled oysters, basket of fries, three fish sandwiches on rye, and a pitcher of Old Style."

He glanced aside to me. "Gus understands the rules, Hayden. This is deep background. All he's looking to do is to confirm the last time you saw Lana Rae, the last time you encountered Lana Rae. He says you are not a person of interest, or a suspect. They are sure they've got Salvatore, but–"

"But something doesn't feel right." Gus intoned.

"Doug, I'm still not sure about this. I've told Tara I'd try to defend Salvatore."

"Salvatore is hanging himself, Hayden. There's nothing any of us can do to hurt him anymore." Doug poured the beers. "Let's see if we can clean this up and move on. There's another reason."

"What's the reason?"

Gus chimed in. "Some folks in internal affairs at the state police think your cousin Scotty has been covering for Salvatore. You might be able to fix his story, get the heat off his back."

"All right. Okay. But Doug, remember, you're in this story too."

Doug nodded. "I know."

So I told Gus a tale that Doug and I had both forgotten. It was June of '91 . . .

Doug and I had gone out hunting squirrel, remember Doug? The construction site where we worked that summer

was shut down due to a wildcat strike by the pipefitters, so
Dad had told us to not plan on coming in for a few days. "Go
play. Chase some girls. Go hunting. Whatever. Just be ready to
go back to work next week." So we went hunting. Chasing
girls costs money, and for the moment we were not working
so there was no money.

We had gone back through the woods that ran along
the back of the farm and over to the railroad tracks. We
followed the tracks for a while, and then dropped down an
embankment to follow the creek. Some younger kids were
trying to float a boat built of packing pallets and tractor inner
tubes; we watched them sink for a few minutes in three feet
of water, and then headed on downstream. We wouldn't
scare up any game that day.

About a half hour later, we made our way up into the
fields behind Henschel's place, coming up behind the
Trattoria. Old Henschel let us hunt small game when his cows
were in, always let us cut through there to save time. We
made our way up to a stand of trees and settled in. I broke
out some sandwiches, and Doug rolled a joint. It seemed like
a good day to get stoned – no work, no game, nothing but
time on a warm June day. After about an hour of considering
the sky and the trees, we started to pack up to head back
home. We decided to cut back to the main highway across
Henschel's farm, and grab a soda at Salvatore's before we
headed back to the house.

As we walked along the tractor path than ran
between the tree line and a patch of tobacco, I spied someone
moving behind the old pump house behind the store.
Laughter trailed our way. Doug here grabbed me by the arm
and pulled me behind a tree. We hunched behind that giant
elm, same as if we had spied a bear or a deer. Peering around

the tree, I saw Salvatore, his arms wrapped around a woman as they kissed and laughed together. They carried on for several minutes as we watched. Then, a sound came from the house, the sound from hell that was the grandmother. Salvatore held her hand and peaked around the corner of the pump house, and called out "coming Mama!"

Then he straightened himself and headed back to the grocery, his composure restored but his step lively. I looked at Doug, Doug looked at me. And we both looked back around the tree and saw Lana Rae, leaning against the back of the pump house, her arms wrapped around herself and a smile of contentment on her face.

It was the first time we had seen her smile like that.

I hadn't thought about seeing Salvatore and Lana Rae together like that until after I spoke to Tara. Then, it came back in a flood of memories. From the first time Lana Rae had come around, she had an eye for Salvatore. He, of course, had the thin veneer of his restaurant charm, but the way she lingered around him every summer day came back to mind. What we didn't know or didn't see is just speculation, but Doug and I knew one little secret.

We waited about ten minutes, then walked up to the store. I got a couple of Dr. Peppers out of the icebox, Doug paid the tab – Randy was at the register, Danny was at reserve drill. In the back of the store, we thought we heard some shouting but we didn't think any more of it. It was hot and we were unemployed for the day, so we went off to find some beer and a place to swim. We kept what we saw back in the field to ourselves.

"Damn." Gus was talking down to his tie again. "He was sexually involved with her?"

"Gus, from where we stood it sure looked that way. Maybe sexually involved, maybe not, but definitely emotionally involved."

Doug nodded.

"That was June. Was that the last time you saw them together?"

"No Gus, it was not. It was probably the last time we saw them alone like that, but Lana Rae, she was coming around a lot. Now remember, we were not staking out the Trattoria, and we had pretty much given up on Danny. We didn't have a lot of reason to come around. But sometimes you'd see him give her a ride, or she'd stop and help him wash his old pickup truck. They'd stand and chat. Mom saw him once, hanging out by the ice chest with his arm draped around her. I suppose they might have been hooking up in town, but that means that they both had to get free from the watching eyes at home. This is a small county, Gus, and if it happens in Carritherston it makes its way out here too."

"What was your last memory of Salvatore and Lana Rae?"

"That'd be August of '91 ...

Mom and Dad were out of town, off on a cruise with their friends from Texas. Having reign over the house and the trust of my parents, of course I decided to have a party. I picked up two kegs of beer on the way home from the job site in Louisville. By seven o'clock, the driveway and yard was filled with cars and high school kids drawn to free beer and no supervision.

It started to rain at about eleven, and by midnight the last keg had run dry while REM and Hootie and the Blowfish still rumbled forth from the stereo speakers. Kids started to file out, and the rolling party broke up and headed toward town and the allure of greasy breakfast and the time to craft excuses for parents.

By one in the morning, it was still raining. Most of the party had cleared out except for some folks who were staying the night, a few who had just passed out, and couple of guys involved in a marathon billiard game that wouldn't end. I went up to the kitchen and made myself a rum and coke, and surveyed the damage from 100 unsupervised teenagers (it was surprisingly spare). So, I went in the living room to kick back on the couch while the party remnants downstairs played truth or dare.

No sooner had my eyes shut then Mike woke me up.

"Hayden! Hayden." I slowly came to life, and saw Mike looming over me. "Get up! There's some babe at the door wants to see you?"

"Huh? Who?"

"I don't know, but she's soaked and she's smokin' hot! Get up, man."

I slowly made my way up and tried to set myself straight. Behind the couch, Kyle, the kicker on the football team, kept trying to make time with Gina, who kept looking to Mike to get her away from him. Mike helped Gina. I made my way to the door; standing inside, soaked, was Jenny Barnes.

"Hayden?" She said to me with a mix of shock and pleasure, giving me a big, wet hug. "Look how you grew up! Oh, honey, it is pouring outside. I am so sorry to get you up, but I thought she might be here."

"Who?"

"Lana."

Lana. Her sister. "Jenny! You are soaked. Look, go down the hall and I'll get you a towel or something. Now what's wrong?"

"Aren't you sweet? Okay. And," she wringed the water from her hair, "you got something dry I can put one? It's pouring out!"

"Sure, c'mon." We walked down the hallway, and I had to evacuate Ben and Collette from the bathroom, where they were having an intense debate over whether she could hold "it" for him. Lana dried off, and I grabbed a pair of my sweats for her. I couldn't help but glance a bit of her as she took the clothes from the door, with drunken admiration.

Jenny came out to the kitchen and joined Mike, Doug and I at the table. Doug spoke for us all as the most sober representative at the table. "Jenny, what are you doing here? I thought you had left. Married or something."

"Oh, honey, I did leave. Drove up from Mount Washington tonight after Momma called. Lana went missing about nine o'clock, and no one can find her," Jenny continued to dry her hair, "I don't suppose she's been by here?"

We all looked at each other. "No, no," we all replied. We had checked out every girl at the party that night, and Lana wasn't among them. "She hasn't been around. Where else did you check?"

"Mainly we've been calling around. Friends and relatives and such, where she went the last time she ran off. No luck. Momma also called the police, but they say until she's gone for a day they can't do anything." We all sat a minute. "Don't suppose you boys have a drink for a thirsty girl?"

Mike tripped over himself to get to the bar, mixing her a rum and soda. As Jenny sat and drank and flirted with poor Mike, Doug and I considered each other with our eyes. I eyeballed him hard, he nodded to me, and we had agreed. That was how our unspoken code worked.

"Jenny," Doug said, "stay here and get dry. Hayden and I will take a look a couple of places we know."

"Are you sure, Doug honey?" her hand tracing her chest just below her neck.

"Yep. Hayden, can you drive a stick? I'm too wasted to drive. Mike?" Mike looked up from Jenny with a happy, oblivious look. "Be careful before you go kicking off the training wheels, okay?"

Doug and I headed down toward Peytona in his Bronco. The rain had finally quit, but we were still getting wet because Doug had left the topper off and the interior was soaked. As we got to the Vigo Road cutoff, I stopped. "Doug, this time of night we've got three options: she's at Ginsburg's barn; she's over at Dutch's in Franklin County, trying to score drinks; or –"

"– or she's with Salvatore. Yeah, I know. Let's save that one for last, so that we don't have to deal with the fallout."

Half-hour later, we had mud-bogged back to Ginsburg's barn, where the stoners usually hung out and partied on Friday night. Skeeter Ginsburg was still up along with a few of the other stoners. They hadn't seen Lana all day, not since school had let out. A couple of the sophomore girls who got stranded there asked us for a lift out, which we gladly obliged. We dropped them at the back of the country club, and left them to sneak home from there. Next, we headed toward Franklin County and stopped by Dutch's. This was our fathers' tavern, which didn't close until four in the morning. Old Dutch had a habit of letting in the high school girls from Cherokee County without carding, and the cops let him get away with it. We were high school boys and had to take care to not get busted for lurking near there.

I pulled up to the drive-through window and talked to Klausman, the old kraut who worked the package store side of the operation. It'd been quiet that night, he said. Most of the girls were probably out at some kegger in the country, and that he hadn't seen Lana either.

Pulling away from Dutch's, I went a quarter-mile and crossed the county line back into Cherokee County. A set of blue flashers went off in my rear view mirror. "Shit."

"God damn it, Hayden, I said be careful!" Doug laid his head back, shut his eyes, and waited for trouble. I reached in my pocket, pulled out my wallet, and placed both hands on the wheel.

"All righty, boys, let's see the license and registration. You want to know why I stopped you boys, being out so late and all?"

It was my cousin. "Scotty?"

"Hayden?" Scotty sighed. "What the fuck are you doing out here at this time of night? You know we goddamn well watch this place just to catch a bunch of little hard cocks like you rolling around. Who's with you?" He shone his light on Doug.

"Dougie. Figures." he said, sighing as he turned off his flashlight and leaned on the truck, "What are you boys doing out here?"

We explained about Lana Rae going missing again, and Jenny coming to ask for help finding her. "Okay, fine. Got it. Look, guys, you tried to do the right thing, but it is three in the morning and you've been drinking and I don't want to explain to your grandma why I ran you in. Go home. Oh, and

Hayden, I pulled you over because there's mud and turf covering your license tag. Scrape it off, then I'm gonna pretend to give you a field sobriety test, and then you're going to get the hell out of here."

"Yessir."

I went through the counting and pointing and toe-standing that constituted sobriety. Scotty and I walked over to his cruiser, and we leaned and talked for a minute while he wrote my "citation" that would never see light of day. "Hayden, where're you boys headed to now?"

"Home, Scotty, swear to God."

"Don't make promises to God that you can't keep, boy. I know you're not done looking for that girl. Tell me where's next. I'll go check it out for you."

"I can't."

"Want me to run you in?"

Scotty didn't bluff. He would run me in just for lying to him.

"We were headed for Salvatore's. It's on the way home."

"Why? He closed hours ago."

I stared at Scotty, the same stare Doug and I shared when we couldn't speak. Scotty nodded.

"Get home. I'll follow you as far as the store to make sure no one hassles you on the way to the house. Call me Sunday and we'll go fishing. I'll let you know how things turn out. Okay?"

"Yes sir."

"Now get."

We got. Scotty followed us as far as the grocery; as we turned off onto Old Bard's Town, I saw him in the rearview mirror, getting out of his car and walking around the store with his big flashlight.

When we arrived back at the house, the pool hustlers had left, nothing was stolen. Jenny was standing in the kitchen, which she had cleaned, putting up the last of the glasses and packing the last of the trash.

"You boys throw a good party. You're buddy Mike," she continued, "he's passed out on the sofa. Tell him I hope to see him again after he wakes up a little more. He's a cutie."

"We couldn't find her."

"Oh, I know. I bet she's up there with that idiot Italian chef. I just wanted to come to the party. Momma, she worries way too much about a girl. You boys didn't have to run off so quick. So," she smiled, sliding off her sandals, "who wants a shot?"

I looked at Doug. Doug nodded back at me. We both smiled at Jenny. Wherever Lana was, she'd be fine.

The next morning I woke up at about eleven. My head pounded from the tequila and the rum. Ben and Collette were still asleep on the floor at the foot of my bed. Doug had sneaked home at some point, and about five other kids were asleep in the living room. The place was remarkably clean, almost as good as how Mom had left it. I picked my way over people and made it to the kitchen. A plate of biscuits and ham sat there, along with a note:

> *Thanks for the fun night sweetie. You and Doug know how to show a girl a good time. I'll let you know the next time I'm passing through here. Meantime, eat up!*
> *XXOO*
> *Jenny*

PS: Lana came home this morning. Your cousin Scotty dropped her off at the house at about five. I'd left the number here at Momma's. She called to let me know everything's all right. Thanks again!

"So was Lana with Salvatore?" Gus queried, taking little interest in the fish or the beer.

"I don't know, Gus. You'd have to ask Scotty. We didn't go fishing that Sunday; it rained and I went to church to get a little salvation after the previous couple of days. Ask Scotty. You know he's with the state police."

"Actually, I did ask Scotty." Gus flipped through some notes in a little book. "As we built up Lana Rae's file, his name kept coming up. You just confirmed his story – he ran into you two out drinking, you pointed him toward Salvatore's and you guys never talked about it again. That about right?"

We both nodded.

Gus confirmed our story with Mike, who had only a vague recollection of the evening. Getting a call from Gus didn't do wonders for my business partner's mood, especially since Lynn had answered the phone when the cops called. It made things cool between the two of us for a few days. Mike doesn't like drama, and we were getting drawn closer to a high profile killing. I went down to Savannah to take a few days off. Doug took off with the kids for Gulf Shores. I'm guessing that Tara was back in the islands.

Chapter 28

RING. RING. RING.

"Yeah? Huh? Hello?" The clock said three-thirty. I'd been asleep for two hours. Mike and I had closed on the houses, and finalized the purchase of the old Iron Works for the investment group backing our loft project. It was a great day, one that would vault the company forward. Dinner that night at the old Greek place Mike had once worked at on Market Street had turned into a riotous celebration, too much revelry and too much drink. I loaded Mike and Lynn in my car and dropped them and our project foreman off in Prospect. After I got everyone home, I headed back to Vintners Landing.

"Hayden."

"Tara?"

"Mmm-hmm. Did I wake you?"

"Oh yeah. What is it?"

"I need to see Salvatore."

It had been two weeks since I'd seen Tara, and a week since I'd last gone to check on Salvatore. Greene River was a two-hour drive, not counting traffic. Greg had an associate down there with Salvatore at all times, and the security was still there. No one had figured out exactly where Salvatore was hiding until trial, but a television helicopter had followed him from town during one of his check-ins with the court. They knew he was down on the Greene River. I'd take her and be discreet.

"Hayden?"

"Huh? I'm here. Look I need a day to set it up. Can you meet me at the house in Vintners Landing, tomorrow morning early? I'll drive us down there."

"You mean like in three hours?"

"No, the next morning after this morning. Tomorrow. You are going to show up this time, right?"

The dial tone in my ear was all the answer I got.

I spent most of the day with the architects we had hired for the Iron Works project. Mike had a vision, but we didn't have the draftsmen necessary to craft plans on this scale. The sessions were fruitful, and they would be back to us in a few weeks with a set of plans for our approval. I'm assuming that they got it right, because my head was not in the meeting.

The next morning, I got up early and went for a run up to the state park and back. The weather was cool, humid, and the sun was barely peeking over the ridgeline as I made my way back to the house.

Tara's little Audi was sitting in the driveway out front.

I went in the house, and she was in the kitchen.

"Hey you. I made some breakfast. Get a shower and then we'll go?"

"Okay. Ten minutes." On again, off again, was on again. I made my way to the shower, got dressed and hustled my way back out to the kitchen. A plate of hot country everything was waiting on the table.

"You got any vodka?"

"Freezer. Why?"

"I need a bloody if I'm going to see Mother." Miss Angina was still at Greene River with Salvatore and their sister, Lenore. "I hope you'll understand."

I didn't. "Of course. Tabasco is in the fridge by the tomato juice. Maybe I should drive?"

"Sure honey."

The sun came out, and Tara made me put down the top on my car. The beauty of the river really shows in the spring and summer, when the leaves have come in. In February, the trees haven't even budded and the wildlife is largely hiding. It's all yellow and gray and brown.

The cabin Greg had secured for Salvatore was really a lodge. Built by an affluent senior partner in the firm as his getaway, it could sleep twenty and had a restaurant-scale full kitchen. Great glass windows offered an unobstructed view of the river and the lake beyond.

When we arrived, the security guards checked us in and cleared us with the associate staying at the house. They knew us both by sight, but they followed procedure like real pros. Greg was back in Miami at trial and wouldn't return until late in the afternoon. Discovery on Salvatore's trial was not going well. The one tell-tale fingerprint, in Lana Rae's blood, on the inside of the wrappings she was found in, established that he had contact with the body. The history indicated an improper relationship. Against the advice of his lawyer, Salvatore had consented to a DNA test, and it had come back showing that he was a match to the other blood found with the corpse, and to the little fetal bones found with Lana Rae. She was pregnant, the baby had been his. All the rest would be conjecture.

Tara went to the back deck and sat with Salvatore. Lenore and Miss Angina were not up yet. I visited with the lawyer. We discussed no details of the case, other than what had been happening in discovery and would be known to the world soon enough. But the lawyer had other worries to share. When the news about the DNA evidence came in, Miss

Angina and Lenore were very upset with Salvatore. Angina had been drinking pretty much the entire time she was at Greene River, and Lenore couldn't control her all the time. The more she drank, the less coherent she became.

"Mr. Rollin," the counselor spoke to me, *sotto voce*, " They keep talking about the same thing. The death of someone named Danny, and what Salvatore could have done and how Salvatore had killed Danny. The mother yells, Salvatore storms out of the room, the mother cries, and the sister tries to pick up the pieces. Every morning is breakfast in silence, every afternoon is civil enough, and every night the soap opera starts up again."

"Let's just stay out of the way, don't you think Ed?"

I stayed in the great study with the lawyer while Tara reacquainted with her family. Looking around, I noticed for the first time all the hunting trophies.

"Ed?"

The lawyer looked up from the brief he was working on. "Yes sir?"

"Are there guns in this house?"

"Yes. Oh. They're locked in a gun cabinet, and the security guy keeps the key. Mr. Borenko already thought about that sir."

"Good. Thanks."

As I glanced out the back window, Tara and Salvatore embraced. They were crying, and happy, at least for the moment. Lenore had gotten up and was padding around the kitchen, and Miss Angina soon followed. She spent most of her days in her housecoat, the lawyer said, just surviving the hours until she could open a bottle of vodka when the sun got to the west side of the house.

They didn't need me, so I logged on the computer and accessed the company server to start looking over some renderings for the Iron Works. The paralegals came down from the city each day; one brought coffee.

Out the doors to the study, I spied Tara and Lenore, together in the kitchen. We had never talked about her sister, but whatever bad I had assumed was in the relationship wasn't evident. They seemed very comfortable with each other, very natural, genuinely happy to be back together. Miss Angina stayed at the table, unmoved, unmoving. Then she left for her room, I assumed to get ready for the day. It was as if her youngest daughter did not exist.

I stayed in the study for most of the afternoon, on the phone with Mike and working through the renderings for the project. Out in the great hall of the lodge, the family reunion continued. Lenore and Salvatore and Tara were together, evidently telling stories and enjoying each others' company, three siblings together. Lenore had divorced her husband a few years back, when the abuse became too much. She decided to stand strong, and stand for herself, and went back to Mobile from Italy. She had not ever met Tara's husband Daemon.

Miss Angina reappeared for lunch at one o'clock. Tara came to the study, and lightly knocked.

"Hayden? Lenore and Salvatore and I wish you'd join us for lunch. Come on."

"Thank you. I will."

It was nice enough to eat outside, so we lunched on the deck looking down toward the lake. Lenore had prepared a light meal, *panzanella* to start, and a fish soup, *cacciucco alla livornese*. The conversation was as light as the meal, focused on me, the family, my book, the project I was working on. Had I met Daemon? *No, but I hear he's a heck of a guy.* What about my wife? *Dead.* So sorry. We made the required journey through the propriety of southern condolences on the way to dessert.

Miss Angina joined us at the end of the meal. She had eaten in the kitchen, and based on past history, had made it a liquid lunch. She didn't speak through dessert, but instead just stared off into the distance, past Tara, past me.

Lenore tried to prompt her into the conversation, but Miss Angina was unmoved. She was not quite as disconnected as when Danny had died, but the strain of watching the life of another of her children unravel was at work.

Lenore cleared the dishes. I got up to help. The words came at my back like a knife.

"Your family is nothing but grief and trouble."

"Mother!"

"Mother!"

"Mother!"

Miss Angina continued. "You watch out for them, these Rollins and Dixons. They help you out, they say you are their friend. Then, when you need them, they are not there. They are never there. Your grandfather left me in jail when I needed him, and you didn't try to save my Danny. Now here you are, tied up in the life of my son and my baby daughter. Why can't you people just go away?"

In another time, and another place, I would have been arrogant and callow, and spoken my mind then and there. I had not kept my tongue when I disagreed with my elders as a child. But, I also knew better now than to be baited. Papaw always said you can't win an argument with an irrational woman, and you can't knock out a drunk. I fell back on those words, and just left the room, and returned to the study and closed the door.

Tara and Salvatore and Lenore and Miss Angina argued for a good hour. Tara left the fight first, walking off into the woods along the river, visibly upset. She couldn't very well leave without me, so I gave her space. Lenore and Angina argued for a while as Salvatore looked on – then Miss Angina took to her room, leaving Lenore and Salvatore in quiet conversation. They had played this scene before, and just stood together, nothing left to say because there was nothing left to do.

Around dusk, Tara made her way back to the lodge. Another quiet knock came on the study door.

"Hayden?

"Mm-hmm." I kept at my work.

"I need to go home. Take me home. Please."

"Sure."

Ten minutes later, we were driving up the highway, with darkness setting in and a cool wind blowing on us. The flurries started soon after, but I kept the top down. I was hoping for the clouds to break, to show me a star.

Two hours later we were back Cherokee County. Tara hadn't spoken the whole drive up. She slept, resting her head on the console, snuggled up under my overcoat.

We rolled past the Trattoria. It was still locked up, but the front windows were boarded up where some punk had tossed bricks through the windows. I noticed one of the guys from the Esso station, out sweeping the parking lot.

We were almost to the house when my phone rang.

"Hayden! It's Greg. Where are you?"

"I'm back home, with Tara. We just turned onto Old Bard's Town Road."

"She's still with you? Good! Turn around and head for Jewish Hospital. Salvatore's mother collapsed and they're taking her to Louisville."

I turned the car around in the middle of the highway and gunned the engine, headed back through Vintners Landing and then west down the Vintners Landing Road. "What the hell happened, Greg?"

Tara stirred when I whipped the car around. "Huh? What happened, Hayden?"

"Hang on and I'll tell you." Her phone rang. I picked up my conversation with Greg while she answered. "What happened?"

"Well, the old lady has been hitting the vodka especially hard, and evidently whatever argument you guys had today must have really set her off. She knocked off a liter of vodka and maybe some pills too. They found her not five minutes after I got to the cabin. She's on a medivac helicopter, and I'm driving Salvatore and Lenore up to the city. I'll be there in about 90 minutes, but you can get there quicker with Tara. Hayden?"

"Yes?"

He was whispering now. "*Hurry. And see if she wakes up, get her to talk. She was muttering something that didn't make sense, but it might just save Salvatore. If he won't save himself, maybe she can.*"

We got on the interstate and cut through the light, westbound traffic. Lenore had called Tara to tell her what was going on. Tara called her personal physician to get to Jewish and get to her mother. We were downtown in about thirty minutes, and caught all the lights to the old hospital on Flexner.

Private hospitals have valet service at the emergency room. I didn't know that until we pulled up. I tossed the keys to the attendant and we rushed in, seeking an information desk. The volunteer directed us to the emergency trauma center, where Tara identified herself as next of kin. The nurse took her back to the room where the doctors were working on Miss Angina. I went out front and called Greg, and waited for him to arrive with Salvatore and Lenore.

It would be almost two hours before they arrived. A state patrol car stopped them northbound on the interstate doing 100 mph, and Greg had to work mightily to get the officer to let him go only with a citation instead of arresting him for reckless driving and impounding his Jaguar. When they pulled in, I hustled Salvatore and Lenore back to the trauma ward and the nurse took them back to Miss Angina.

Greg and I had nothing to do but wait. After about a half-hour, the first television van showed up. They lingered near us, but did not recognize either of us. They made inquiries to the information desk, which indicated that they could talk to the public affairs officer at eight in the morning when she arrived. Another camera crew arrived, then a third, followed by the police beat reporter who hung around the Franklin Avenue precinct. He sidled up by Greg and me. "Mr. Borenko? It's Cliff Hudson from the *C-J*. Is your client here?"

"Cliff?" Greg inquired.

"Yes sir?"

"I will answer three questions if you will do two things. Go the hell away, and take those televised boobs with you."

"Deal. First question: Is your client Salvatore Lichten here?"

"Yes."

"Did he try to kill himself?"

"No, he did not. He is the rosy bloom of health."

"Who is hospitalized that brings him here?"

"His mother. Now go away."

Cliff turned to me. "Mr. Rollin?"

Greg stopped him. "Go away now Cliff, before Hayden kicks your ass."

After Cliff had gone, and taken his camera-toting colleagues with him, Greg filled me in on what happened. The argument between Lenore and Salvatore and Miss Angina had started up again after dinner. The old woman went off, alone, and was throwing back vodka and evidently mixing it with the sleeping pills a doctor had prescribed for her. They found her passed out, covered in vomit, and non-responsive. They were able to get her wake enough and breathing, and called 911.

"She was muttering something, about a letter, a letter about Danny and Salvatore that she wrote. You know anything about that? Anything? The way she was talking, it sounded like she was back at his funeral. She kept talking about who Danny killed, who Danny killed."

"You mean who killed Danny? Tyler Bridges killed Danny. He had to do it. He was the deputy who had the shot."

"No, she said *who Danny killed.*"

"Danny didn't hit anyone that night. No one else was killed."

"You think –"

"Yes, yes I do. Now we need to prove it."

Around midnight, Tara came out from the trauma ward. Her makeup was lined from tears, hair unkempt.

"Momma's gone. Miss Angina's gone. I –"

Tara collapsed in one of the chairs, sobbing. Lenore and Salvatore were still in back. Greg went off to be with the client. I sat with Tara. She must have cried for fifteen minutes, twenty, gasping and unable to speak.

"I don't want to go that way. So sad. So unhappy. You know she was beautiful, once."

"I know."

"She loved you Hayden. She loved all of your family. You were good friends, good family. Even when she hated you, she really loved you."

"I know. Are you okay?"

"I just need to sit. I need to sit here, alone. Then I need to talk to you about something. Something Miss Angina said. You'll need to take care of it. Please. Salvatore won't help himself. You do this thing. Save my brother."

Two hours later, I drove her straight home to Gilliam's Point. As we headed up the winding drive, she told me what Miss Angina had said. I listened, nodded. I understood. Tara kissed me lightly, stroked my beard, and got out of the car.

"Now go take care of it Hayden."

Chapter 29

TWO DAYS LATER, GREG, DOUG, and I sat in the office of Trey Lawson at the commonwealth attorney's office, housed in the new county justice center for the 53rd circuit over in Shelby County. The young prosecutor looked at us both in disbelief.

"You want to what?"

"I want you to exhume the body of Daniel David Cahill." Greg handed him the motion.

"Why in the world would I exhume that body? Why is the body of a guy who was killed in a shootout with the police twenty years ago of any consequence to this case?"

Doug went to speak, but Greg interrupted. "We have it on good authority that there is evidence in the casket relevant to the murder you are preparing to prosecute. It is in everyone's interest that the body be exhumed. It is in the interest of justice."

Trey leaned forward in his chair. He was all starchy angles, from his flattop and his square jaw to his little bow tie and his pressed chinos. "Wait a minute. This is the half-brother of the man I'm trying. If the evidence is there, and it is so important, have your client as next of kin agree to the exhumation. You don't need me."

"Well," Greg said, "that's the problem. Mr. Lichten is unwilling to approve the exhumation. In fact, it has been generally difficult to get him to cooperate in his own defense. Dr. Rollin here arranged for most of his defense, and to the extent anyone has been able to fill in facts related to this case, it has been from his efforts to compel cooperation."

Trey turned to me. I had played church league ball with his older brother, Trip. "Hayden, what's your interest in this case?"

"I'm just an old friend of the family. His brother was my friend, and I know it is what he would want me to do – to help his brother. But, we have reached the point where he is impeding his own defense. It is as if he wants to die. All of the physical and circumstantial evidence points to him as the man who killed Lana Rae Barnes. But there is something not right with the story – something just doesn't quite fit. He's made no effort to explain his whereabouts to the police or his own counsel."

"Are you sure your perceptions are not distorted by your closeness to the case? I believe you were involved with his sister? Or are involved, perhaps?"

"Look, Trey, maybe I am suffering some perception problems. But if you listen to either of these lawyers, neither of whom is emotionally tied to the case, they will tell you the same thing. There is information in that coffin that has bearing on this case. Do you want to just get a conviction, or do you want to get it right? As it stands, you're about to send the wrong man to Eddyville."

Trey stared out the window. As an assistant commonwealth's attorney, his reputation as a successful prosecutor was well established. He had political ambitions. How those ambitions were served by this case was not certain. We sat and watched him for moments, minutes, time passing slowly.

"Convince me."

It was Doug's turn.

"Trey, consider the following. A prosecutor is the power of the commonwealth. As commonwealth's attorney, you have tremendous power, the power to investigate and convict, in order to protect the people of the commonwealth. If the man on trial is guilty, then it is necessary to convict him not just because the weight of evidence says convict, but also because that conviction in fact makes the commonwealth safer, and it serves justice."

Doug continued. "If, however, that man is innocent, and the power of the commonwealth's attorney office puts him there despite the strong suspicion that there is another candidate for conviction, despite the presence of a strong alternate theory, despite the existence of evidence that the alternate theory is true, then your office failed to protect the Commonwealth."

"Why?"

"Because, Trey, justice is not served. In a capital offense, it is incumbent on your office to disprove a strong alternative theory. And, further, given Mr. Lichten's unwillingness to engage in his own defense, we will have to move to have him declared incompetent and an impediment to his own defense, and we'll get any conviction thrown on appeal. Then we'll do the whole thing all over again, but this time there will be a conservator appointed to act on behalf of his family and estate, and the first thing they will do is sign off on exhuming that body."

Now Greg came at him. "Trey, you and I tangled before. You know I will do this. And I know that you are more than a reasonable man – you're an honorable man and you won't be able to live with yourself if you send up an innocent man. All I'm asking for is a backhoe and a preacher, and that you are there with the rest of us when that casket gets unsealed. We can test our theory then and there – you, me, Doug, and the judge."

Trey picked up the phone. "Lee? Yeah. Call Judge Davis and tell him that Mr. Borenko and I are coming over in an hour, if he can make room on his schedule. And send me in a paralegal – I need to draft a motion."

"Greg, Doug, let's put it on paper and see what the judge says. Hayden, is it safe to assume you know someone with a backhoe who I can get on short notice?"

As it happened, I did.

Chapter 30

THE JUDGE HAD HEARD THE MOTION in chambers, and agreed to grant the order. Paul Davis was sixty and looking forward to a quiet last year on the bench. He had already decided to not stand for reelection, and instead return to his partnership fulltime and rake in fees doing quiet arbitration work. He enjoyed pontificating on the joy of doing justice from the bench, and in this instance he saw through the screen and seized on the chance. As a good liberal, he hated to see an innocent man go to jail; as a former prosecutor, he hated to see the guilty walk free. In this instance, he got to help someone who would not help themselves. Greg backing Trey's request (made at Greg's urging) in the name of justice seemed to resonate with the man.

An hour later we were at the old graveyard at the Grove Hill Cemetery in Carritherston. My uncle Caleb had been waiting with a backhoe and my second cousin Clay, the Cherokee County coroner, had come out to supervise the expected exhumation. Trey had called Gus Ellis, who in turn had called the Kentucky State Police crime scene unit to meet up with the assistant commonwealth's attorney and the accompanying court order. I had also taken the time to call Cecil Boatwright, the family's preacher. Danny would have to be reburied after the exhumation, and a proper Christian relaying of his remains was the least I could do.

The blade of the hoe cut deep into the fertile soil. Two cuts, three, four, and a pile of dark loam formed to the left of the grave. Soon the blade met the top of the concrete tomb. Two undertakers cleared away the dirt from the top of the tomb, and attached a strap to the two steel eyehooks in the top, and attached them to the teeth of the backhoe blade.

Caleb lifted the top off the tomb, leaving it to rest on the earthen pile, and pulled the backhoe away.

The two undertakers wheeled over a coffin crane and quickly had it set up over the gravesite. The younger undertaker, wiry and not more than twenty-five, jumped into the grave and fished the straps of the crane underneath the coffin. After he climbed out, the older undertaker started the battery winch and started to raise the coffin from the grave. As it cleared the surface of the ground, they ran two four-by-fours under the coffin, and then lowered it to rest on the beams.

Then the older man placed the coffin key in the crank house of the coffin and slowly unsealed it. A rush of gas passed from the coffin as it opened. Gus and the crime scene unit investigator moved close, looking in as the coffin lid was removed.

There was Danny, or at least the mummified remains of Danny. He had withered over the years, but the cap was still perched on his head, his arms crossed across the breast of his jacket coat.

Trey looked at Greg. Greg nodded to Trey, who motioned to the detective. Gus reached inside the right breast pocket with a gloved hand, then again into the left breast pocket of the coat, and produced a yellowed envelope.

"This it?" He passed the envelope to Trey. The prosecutor looked at the back of the envelope, which was sealed and signed with a signature and a date. Photographs were taken of the scene by the forensics team, and the envelope was photographed, dusted, and scanned and then placed in a plastic evidence bag.

The crime scene unit worked for a good hour, collecting physical evidence from the body and also carefully going over the remains and the coffin for any other surprises. There was nothing out of the ordinary for a recently unearthed body.

Danny's remains were placed back in order. The undertakers resealed the coffin. Cecil pronounced a brief funeral oration, asking God for forgiveness for disturbing the sleep of the dead, but also asking for understanding that to do so might save the soul of the living, or at least allow all souls to lay at rest. I went over and turned the handle on the coffin crane, laying Danny to rest one last time. As Caleb filled in the grave, I walked back to my car with Doug. Greg stayed with Trey, in order to ensure the chain of custody for this new, unread evidence. We headed back downtown as the setting sun cut through the overcast and burned our eyes with a brief hint of the spring yet to come.

Chapter 31

THE PARCHMENT WAS OLD AND DRIED AND YELLOW. The ink was blue, a bit faded but entirely legible. The handwriting was delicate, that of a lady, but in a shaky hand:

November 19, 1991

Dear Lord,

I am writing this letter as a prayer to you to forgive the soul of my youngest son. He bears the burden of my sins, and the sins of his brother, and the sins of his grandmother.

My Danny is dead because of all of our sins. The truth has never been spoken, to the police, or even outside our family, because the shame was too great to bear. It is only now, before I go to bury my baby, before I go myself, that the truth is clear in my mind. Lord, please forgive me for ruining my children, for ruining my life, and please dear God make them whole. Especially my baby boy, who I send to you.

He died at the hand of a police officer, which is no justice for the world because he had committed no crime. He's dead because of a whore, an accident, and a crime of passion. I had no idea what had happened until four days ago, when my sons argued and fought and one of them died. Danny died for the sins of his brother. He was driven to those sins by my own selfishness and my mother's ruthless hand that stripped away his identity as a man. He died protecting me from my own weakness. I killed that woman, and my boys hid the fact to protect me.

Danny died because he repaired the weakness of his brother Salvatore. Salvatore's weakness came because I couldn't protect him and his grandmother destroyed his will. They fought. Danny died.

Danny and Salvatore, they protected me, Danny and his brother did. And when he protected me, and protected Salvatore, he took the life of another person. He killed to protect his brother from a demon in the guise of a girl. Lana Rae seduced my son Salvatore, tricked him into bed and said she had his child. She threatened our family and threatened my older boy. Salvatore wasn't strong, and he wasn't willing to stand up to her. When Mother confronted them both, Lana fled and Salvatore chased her, but he couldn't find her.

I didn't know what happened until four nights ago, but now I know, and I have to tell you. Danny and Salvatore's battle brought back my memories. I was drinking – I've always been weak for drink, you know – and I ran over Lana. Ran over her and killed her, thought I killed her dead. My boys, they cleaned up after me, they let me forget. But now I know, and I know that what I did made my one boy a killer.

I didn't know that Danny saw what happened with Salvatore and Lana. He followed Lana and he beat her and killed her. None of us but Salvatore knew until the night Danny was killed. His guilt had made him irrational, and when he and Salvatore fought each other that night, it was because Danny's guilt had gotten the best of him. He wanted to go to the police, he wanted to confess that he killed that little lying whore. God had gotten into his heart and told him he had done wrong. Salvatore wouldn't let him go, wouldn't let Danny bear the burden of his crime. Salvatore wouldn't let Danny expose what I had done. They fought, and when Danny tried to stab Salvatore, the cold fury in his eyes showed he was gone. He fled into his apartment. That was the last time I saw him alive on this earth.

I am still not able to speak of what happened. My only hope, dear Lord, is that writing to you will set my mind at ease and allow me to walk in this world. I have failed all boys so miserably, and now there is nothing left to do but ask you to forgive them both.

I ask your forgiveness. Please.

Your daughter,

Angina

"So Angina is the mother of our suspect?"

"Sir," Gus addressed Trey, "that would be correct."

"Where is she?"

"Dead." Doug volunteered. "Early this morning. And she tried to kill herself the night after the brother's funeral in 1991. Sleeping pills. No permanent damage, but she damned near put herself in the ground forever. She died last night, seizure brought on from too much alcohol and too many pills. The last thing she did was make a statement to her granddaughter that this letter existed, and that it would save Salvatore."

"It's a deathbed testament." Greg quietly prodded Trey. "She wrote this the last time she tried to commit suicide, and put it in the coffin. And now she made deathbed testimony again to take us to this evidence."

The commonwealth's attorney contemplated for a moment. Finally, he turned to Gus. "Ellis, I want to verify the handwriting on that document. The DMV should have a signature on that woman that we can use for comparison. Then, run the DNA again, this time against the hair samples we pulled from the corpse. See if there's a hit on anything from Lana Rae. That'll give us enough physical evidence to wrap up the homicide."

"So you'll be dropping charges against Mr. Lichten?" Greg inquired.

"Not quite, counselor. Mr. Lichten has been part of a conspiracy to cover up a homicide. And vehicular homicide in Kentucky is a serious felony, and it has no statute of limitations."

"But the statute of limitations for conspiracy –"

The prosecutor interrupted Greg. "– is one year in Kentucky, I know. And the homicide is over fifteen years old. But the conspiracy has been ongoing. Mr. Lichten is unwilling to cooperate in clearing up these facts. The charge will stand. But that is on top of his far larger problem."

"What problem?"

"Lana Rae Barnes was pregnant. DNA evidence ties him to the fetal remains. He had sex with a minor female, got her pregnant. Under the Commonwealth code section 510. 020, when a person over 21 has sex with someone sixteen or under, that constitutes third degree rape under the statutory rape laws. There is no statute of limitations under the laws of the Commonwealth for any form of rape including statutory rape. He's still looking at five years in prison."

Doug chimed in again. "Now I think you have a problem, Trey."

"Do tell counselor. I'm all ears." Trey stared at Doug, unblinking.

"Under the law of the Commonwealth, you are tried under the law that applies at the time the act occurred. To do otherwise is to apply an ex post facto standard on a previous act. If Mr. Lichten did have sexual relations with Lana Barnes when she was sixteen, then there is no statutory rape according to Kentucky law. And, if the timeline in this letter is correct – it corroborates the physical evidence of the fetal bones – then she was seventeen when they slept together. The age of consent in Kentucky in 1991 was sixteen or older. Unless you can prove that Mr. Lichten actually had intercourse with that girl more than a year before she was killed, I don't think you have a case. You have a genetic match, but that could come from Danny too. And, for all we know, she was playing them both."

"So," Greg took up the banner, "unless you want to spend all the time and money it will take to run down eye witnesses from more than fifteen years ago who can offer proof beyond a reasonable doubt that Salvatore was sexually involved with the Lana Rae before she turned sixteen, I am afraid you really don't have a case. And, even then, the statute of limitations ran out on statutory three years ago. Now, do you want to talk about the conspiracy charge and see if we can clear this mess up once and for all?"

Trey slumped back in his chair, took off his horn-rimmed spectacles and rubbed the bridge of his nose. "Get him to allocute to the conspiracy charge. He has to describe what happened to Lana Barnes, how he found out, what he did. He has to corroborate the facts in this letter, in open court. I'll ask for a suspended sentence on the conspiracy in exchange. But if he ever so much as smiles too nicely at a woman under seventeen, we'll land on him. He's under a microscope. One step out of line, and he's off to do five years in Eddyville. I will find something to put him there."

Chapter 32

JUDGE DAVIS HAD AGREED TO A CLOSED HEARING to take Salvatore's allocution statement. Greg Borenko took Salvatore through his statement, with Doug as his co-counsel. Trey Lawson sat to represent the commonwealth. The transcript of the statement would be submitted to the court with his plea on conspiracy charges. The judge allowed Tara and me to sit in on the hearing, representing the family.

"Salvatore," Greg began, "the letter from your mother that was in Danny's grave makes it clear that you didn't kill Lana Rae. Now, in order to dismiss this, I am going to need you to explain to us what did happen to her."

"Well, there are really two stories here. One is of what happened to Lana Rae, how she was killed and ended up in that hillside. The other is about how Danny got killed."

"Danny was killed by the police." Greg prompted. "Danny was shooting at the police and they shot back and killed him."

"Yes, yes, this is so. But Lana Rae wouldn't be dead, and Danny wouldn't be dead, if it wasn't for me, or for Mother. Mother and Mama raised me to look after Danny, to protect him from himself. I tried to do that as long as I could, but when he got involved in the drugs, when he became a teenager, it was too hard. He didn't want to listen; he developed his own sense of justice. But when Momma killed Lana, we couldn't do anything except protect her. The scandal would have been too great."

Trey looked up, stunned. "Your mother killed Lana Rae Barnes? I'm confused Mr. Lichten. What does your mother have to do with Lana Rae?"

"Mother killed Lana Rae. Or, at least, I thought she did. Danny thought she did. And we acted to try and protect Mother. She was so weak, so very weak and she needed people to look out for her."

Greg and Trey traded looks of bemusement. Greg went back to guiding Salvatore through his statement. "Salvatore, just go ahead and walk Trey through the events. Are we back on the record now, right?"

The court reporter nodded.

Greg resumed questioning. "So Salvatore, please walk us through the events that led to the death of Lana Rae Barnes."

"Lana had been coming around the restaurant ever since her family moved in over there on Old Bard's Town Road. Her older sister, well, she was a slut, always throwing herself at boys and hanging out of her clothes that way. But Lana, well, Lana was different. She was mature, and thoughtful. She liked beautiful things. She liked to talk. I always imagined she was like what Tara would have been like if she had been around. I liked her company. She needed someone to act like a good brother to her, to guide her."

"Is that how you got involved with her? You saw the relationship as fraternal, or avuncular?"

"She'd come around and buy things for her momma, or the kids would be hanging around out front and she'd come around while I was working the meat counter, and just talk. She just likes to talk. And we'd visit. She liked my cooking, and she would keep me company in the kitchen when I'd prepare the *gastronomia*. She liked the photographs I'd take when I'd go walking on Sundays. She'd listen. But she had problems at home. Her father, well he drank. So did my father, and my mother, and my step-fathers. I knew what it was like to handle that, so I'd listen to her. Counsel her. Tell her how to survive and how to hide while inside herself. Mostly, I listened. Anyhow, for a year or so, she'd just come around and visit and talk, but there wasn't anything else to it."

"What changed?"

"When she was fifteen, she ran away from home for the first time. She came knocking on the storehouse door late at night, all crying and upset. I let her sleep in the storehouse, and then she took off the next day. I didn't give her any money or anything, told her that she could stay but that she ought to go home and try to make things work."

"Did she do that?"

"Yes. She wasn't in the storeroom the next day, and later that week she and her sister came walking up the road from down by the railroad tracks. I'm guessing so."

"And when exactly was that?"

"June, 1989."

"Just before they moved away for a while."

"Yes."

Greg stopped and consulted his notes for a moment, took a drink of water.

"So what happened that brought you and Lana Rae back together?"

Salvatore continued his statement. "Well, in the spring of 1991 Barnes and his wife moved back up. And they brought Lana back. Jenny had run off and gotten married, so she wasn't around as much. But Lana was back, and she'd come to visit. She had grown up, and she was pushing on me a lot more. Momma and Mama –"

"Mama?"

"Grandmother, Mama Kessler. Mother and Mama, they both noticed, and they got all concerned. Mama and I had the most awful arguments about her. She wouldn't let me near her in the store or around the grounds, always shushed me off somewhere if she saw Lana Rae coming."

"So what did you do?"

"Well, she was seventeen by then, and she wanted to be together. I'd sneak out into the back field on breaks, or late at night, and she'd be there. We'd walk, or talk, or maybe take a drive. Eventually, we started to become physically involved. She wanted to make love, and so did I. And we did."

"When was that?"

"July 1991."

"How long did this go on?"

"Until she left, ran off again in September."

"September 1991?"

"Yes."

"When is the last time you were with her?"

"August 18, 1991."

"What happened on August 18, Salvatore?"

"It had been a hot, hot week. That night, thunderstorms broke out all over the place, and we were getting poured on all day. Just after I had closed up the store, I went upstairs and did the books. I was home alone. Mother was in Texas visiting my sister Lenore, and Mama had gone to bed early with a summer cold. Danny was away at weekend drill for Reserves. Anyhow, I was upstairs finishing the books when I heard this knock at the back door, by the storehouse. It was Lana."

"What happened next, Salvatore?"

"Well Mr. Borenko, she said she was running off, and not coming back. Her father had tried to do something,

something she didn't want to do, and she had run off. But, she wanted me to go, because she was pregnant. She said it was mine, and she wanted to be with me and wanted to make a family. But I had to protect her and go with her. So I took her in, and dried her and we ate and we talked, talked late into the night. We fell asleep over in the kitchen of the Trattoria, sitting on the floor."

Greg prodded him. "She didn't stay?"

"No. At about four o'clock I heard engines outside. I saw Hayden and Doug leaving the parking lot in Doug's truck. But, there was also a police cruiser. I figured maybe those boys had a little trouble coming home and they'd been pulled over. But then the officer started walking around back to the storehouse door, and started knocking. Now, I'm afraid he'll wake Mama, so I ran through the storehouse and got the door."

"Was it an officer?"

"Yes. It was Scotty. Now, Scotty and I went to school together, and he's standing there with his big flashlight and he says, 'Salvatore, you know who I'm looking for, and you know why. Tell her to come on out, and let's figure this thing out so you don't get in any more trouble than you have too.' I tell Scotty to go around to the east end of the building, and we'll meet him there. He does, and I get Lana up and tell her to go outside. She was unhappy, but Scotty sat with her and heard her story, then told her not to worry. He works up a story that he found her walking near Carritherston, and calls the mother and lets her know she's okay. The father's gone, had a fight with the mother after Jenny had come home and confronted the father. So Lana can come home. Next day, Scotty brings county family services out and they start working to keep the father away."

"Your name never came up?"

"As far as I know."

"Now, what does this have to do with her murder? And with your Mother. You say Miss Angina killed her?"

"Lana kept coming around, keeping after me to run off with her. But now Mother and Danny were both back, and Mama was feeling better. She knew something was wrong. So anyhow, Lana comes around, wanting to leave, wanting me to go with her. It's the middle of September, September 17. We're in the field, behind the old pump house and there's a big bright moon. She says either I need to take her away, or she's going to my family about the baby. Then she left, ran off toward Henschel's field."

Trey Lawson interjected. "That's the last time you saw her alive?"

"Yes sir."

Lawson again. "September 17."

"Yes, sir."

Greg resumed the questioning. "What were you going to do, Salvatore?"

"I didn't know. Pray. Decide. But I never got the chance."

"Why not?"

"Well, she ran far, real far, and headed down the tracks. All the kids have walked those tracks – they are a path and a trail, but they're isolated and private at the same time. You know where you're going. Anyhow, Mother had been in Frankfort, out drinking with friends she knew, and she was headed home late. And, as usual, she'd had too much to drink, way too much to drink. She's coming up the old road from Waddy, and I guess she saw Lana walking along the road, just past the tracks. Don't know if Mother saw Lana or not, but it doesn't really matter now, I guess. They're both dead. Mother ran over Lana in the Mercedes, knocked her yards off the road and then spun off into the ditch on the other side of the old road. Maybe thirty minutes later she called the house and said she'd had an accident and couldn't drive. So Danny and I took the pickup and went to find her."

"Go on."

"When we got there, the Mercedes was fine, but the front windshield was broken and there was blood on the front of the car. I don't know if there were skid marks or not. But, the Mercedes wouldn't start; we'd need to pull it in. I had Danny run Mother home, and I pushed the Mercedes off to the side of the road and waited for him to come back. Maybe twenty minutes later, he was back. I was looking for one of the hubcaps that had flown off the Mercedes, looking for whatever Mother had hit. As I was walking back down the road toward the tracks, Danny's headlights came up on me and illuminated something in the scrub off the side of the road."

"What was it?"

"It was Lana Rae. She wasn't moving. I ran over, and yelled to Danny for help. She wasn't breathing. As far as I could tell she was dead. I was crying, stunned. I don't know if any of you understand the feeling of loss that comes when the one thing you love is ripped away, so violently and randomly."

"Why didn't you call the authorities?"

"The scandal would have been too much for Mother. Mama, she could have stood it, but not Mother. She's so fragile. *She was so fragile.* So I started thinking, where could I lay her to rest? The construction crews working on the old trestle had been coming for sandwiches at lunch, and I knew they were going to backfill where the new embankment was the next morning. I got some butcher paper and plastic from the back of the truck, and wrapped Lana up real careful and carried her over to the trestle. I knew an old back way, across Merry Dixon's old farm. So I went over there with Danny, and made him help lay her to rest under that train trestle. Then I made him promise to never talk about it again."

"How'd she get stabbed?"

Salvatore looked up, years coming to his eyes. "She hadn't been stabbed when I laid her down. I started to break down. I just couldn't finish. The emotions had overtaken me. Danny sent me back to the truck, told me he'd finish covering her up. He told me to get home to Mother, to look after Mother, that he'd take care of Lana and the Mercedes."

"So you left?"

"I left. I drove the truck back home and tended to Mother, got her cleaned up and to bed. Mama was up, and she only said 'you cannot speak of this again. You know it and I know it. Never again. Go mourn your whore but in the morning, with the sunrise, this is over!'"

"What happened to the Mercedes?"

"Danny got it started, and drove it into a deep part of the Kentucky River where the Fork meets it. Mother reported it stolen the next day. She didn't even remember going to Frankfort. I bet it's still down there."

"So how did Lana get stabbed?"

Salvatore sat, tears coming, trying to gain his composure. He looked straight at Trey.

"I didn't find out until later. Like I said before, Danny was back home from drill. What I didn't know was that earlier that night, he had been back in the field, getting stoned or something. We didn't see him, but he overheard us and watched. When I left, as he was burying her, she stirred. She breathed. Her breath had been so shallow, her pulse so weak, I thought she was dead. Danny, when she stirred, Danny stabbed her with that survival knife I'd given him years ago, and kept stabbing and stabbing and stabbing until she was gone."

"How do you know?"

"The night Danny was shot, it came out. That's when he told me. It's why we fought."

Greg checked his notes, looked at the judge, and then looked at the prosecutor. "Trey, is that good enough?"

"I suppose." Trey checked his notes for a minute. "We'll submit the written statement to the judge, have Salvatore affirm the basic facts, and get the suspended sentence for conspiracy. There's one thing I'd like to know, if Salvatore is willing to talk about it."

Greg replied. "Off the record?"

"Off the record."

The court reporter shut down her machine. Trey motioned for her to leave.

Trey turned to Salvatore. "What really happened the night Danny was killed by the police?"

Salvatore looked to Greg. "Can I tell?"

"Well, Salvatore, did you do anything wrong that night?"

"No."

"Then it is up to you to decide. You have no obligation to speak at this point. Trey, I'll be listening for incriminating remarks, and I'll deny this conversation if you do anything to my client."

"Relax, Greg. Just curious. I think he wants to tell."

Greg told Salvatore to go on.

"Well, the fight that set things off wasn't about the Guard discharge. I knew about it, didn't really care. If he didn't want to serve, he didn't have to. He was a young man, and young men are like that. The problem was, he couldn't handle doing murder. His conscience was getting to him, and he got all worked up and told his mother and grandmother what had happened, told them about everything – Lana Rae, the baby, and the killing. I tried to get him to shut up, but he wouldn't quit. He stormed out of the house and into the Trattoria. When we caught up with him, he wanted to go to the police. His grandmother and mother begged me to get him to stop. Mother, she couldn't even remember what had happened. I hit him, knocked him down. He jumped up, and pulled the same knife he used to kill Lana Rae, told me he'd killed her with it and now he'd do me too. He lunged at me with the knife, and I deflected it with a cutting board. Knocked the knife out of his hand, and slapped him across the face. He bolted, ran into his apartment, and barricaded the doors. The rest of what happened is just like what we told the police that night."

We all sat there, stunned. Salvatore kept going. "All he wanted to do was protect me. All he ever wanted to be was powerful, and able to determine his own destiny. I lost that chance, lost it to Mother's alcoholism and Mama's will. All I ever wanted to do for him was give him a little disciple so that he'd know how to use independence. You didn't need me to clean up this murder, Hayden. I could have borne the burden of it, because I'd already killed Danny. I killed him with my secrets, with my weakness, and because I couldn't make him any better than he was. He couldn't handle the secrets.

"I could never get Danny to understand that there was no glory in what he wanted to do, only pain and destruction made necessary by common need. A man has to accept that he is already dead in order to kill. I'd been dead for years before Lana Rae came along, and that was how I got through days. But then she showed me light, and tenderness, and newness – I'd never known any of that, not when I was young, not later. When it got taken away, I was dead again. But I had to protect the family, protect my brother. She wasn't coming back, she wasn't wanted at home. I would die to protect Danny, even after his death. I would die to protect my Mother, even after her death. And if Hayden had minded his own damned business, this secret would have gone to Eddyville with me and then to my grave. But I know why he did this too, and I think I understand his motive. Maybe, just maybe, now I'll be able to live, though I don't know what for."

I left the room as Greg and Trey and Doug finished the paperwork. Salvatore sat in the chair at the middle of the room, looking down. He looked as though his heart was breaking all over again.

An hour later, Tara met us outside the courthouse. She'd brought a hire car to take Lenore and Salvatore out to Vintners Landing. Salvatore and Lenore talked quietly, removed in time and space and experience from their youngest sister. While her siblings settled in the back of the town car, we walked across the street to my old convertible.

"So," I said to her, "what happens now?"

"First, we have to lay mother to rest. Then Salvatore will go stay with Lenore for a few weeks in Mobile, figure out what to do next, straighten out Miss Angina's estate. You know why he never sold the Trattoria?"

"Why"

"He didn't own it. Mama had left the store in equal shares to Miss Angina, Salvatore, Lenore, and our uncle Amos. All four of them would have to agree to sell, but Miss Angina wasn't willing to let go of the Trattoria. So he had to stay there and tend to it. He could have cooked anywhere, been a success with a great kitchen in a great restaurant in New York or New Orleans. Now, with Miss Angina gone, I suspect we'll turn over the property to some developer. I may go ahead and buy it and bulldoze the store. It's such an awful place, such awful memories for them all. Maybe he can start a new kitchen in Mobile."

We stood for a few minutes more, not really talking, but taking in the winds that carried the faint scent of the coming spring. I went to light a cigarette, but she stopped me. "Don't. The air is clear, and it should stay that way."

"What about you, Tara? What do you do next?"

"I keep going. I have a good life, a good business. You helped me keep out of the papers and to keep my good name, which I will always remember. But I'll keep going."

"And Daemon?"

"Him? Ever hear of 'divorce in the house' where a marriage is kept on paper, but within the house the partners are no longer together? It is bad for business for Daemon and I to break up. He'll have his interests and me, well," she rested a light hand on my arm, "I'll have mine. But I doubt that Daemon and I will see much of each other. It is a big house."

"You know where to find me if you need me."

"Yes. Yes I do. I will. Soon."

Tara turned and walked toward the town car. I climbed into the old pony car, turned over the engine, and put down the top. As I pulled out onto Jefferson Street, I hit the dial button on the phone. In my rearview mirror, I saw her climbing into the back of the town car. She paused, and looked back, her eyes looking back at me. She smiled. The driver shut the door and they rolled away.

I could make choices out of hope, instead of from out of loss. I was by myself, but I wasn't alone.

-Fin-

Postlude

A PAIR OF FRENCH DOORS OPENED ONTO THE GALLERY of the old row house. Five blocks away, on the other side of the levee rising above Uptown, the ships on the Mississippi sound their horns at each other, heading upriver or downriver, and reminding the city that the day is beginning. Below the gallery of the house, down on Constance Street, the sounds of children headed toward the Live Oak School mix with the chattering patois of the working girls headed home and the chirping of the birds in the old oaks, signaling that the Irish Channel has come to life for the day.

Downstairs, the smell of fresh chicory wafts on the humid morning air, making its way up the stairs. Bare feet, bare except for painted toenails and a silver toe ring on the left pinkie toe, pad up the stairs. The oak door to the front bedroom opens.

"Hayden? Hayden? Wake up honey."

"Huh? Five minutes. Just five minutes."

"You sure? You slept hard, all night. You didn't even move after you fell asleep. Now come on, get up. I made you some breakfast; now, tell me the end of the story before I have to leave for seminar."

About the Author

Keith Gaddie is a writer, college professor, and litigation consultant. He and his wife Kim, their four children, and three very large dogs live in Norman, Oklahoma. Keith teaches politics at the University of Oklahoma and is also a news contributor to the local NPR station, KGOU. A native Kentuckian, *Ghosts on Vintners Landing* is his fifteenth book.

Acknowledgments

Thank you to our family and friends who supported us and provided help during our most challenging times. You know who you are. To our praying friends; Gia, Sherry, Anne, Kellie, Brooke, and Sara. Thank you for praying every time I sent you a text!

A very special thank-you to Gia. You know what this life is like (because you live it too). Every step of the way, you provided help and encouragement.

A very special thank-you to Sherry. Your encouragement, prayers and guidance mean so much.

An extra special thank-you to Noah and Lauren for making lemonade out of some pretty bitter lemons.

Thank you to Lesley for your incredible insight and help in turning our story into what it needed to be.

Additional thank-you to Jack Hibbs, J.D. Farag, and David Jeremiah for faithfully teaching truth.

Resources

With so much deception and censorship in our world today, we wanted to give some helpful resources:

Books by Ray Stedman

Books by Charles Stanley

Real Life with Jack Hibbs

J.D. Farag.org

Dr. David Jeremiah.org

JB Hixson.org or notbyworks.org